THE FATE OF
BONTÉ III

ALAIN POISSANT

THE FATE OF BONTÉ III

Translated by Rob Twiss

University of Ottawa Press
Literary Translation Collection

uOttawa

The University of Ottawa Press gratefully acknowledges the support extended to its publishing list by Heritage Canada through the Canada Book Fund, by the Canada Council for the Arts, by the Ontario Arts Council, by the Federation for the Humanities and Social Sciences through the Awards to Scholarly Publications Programs and by the University of Ottawa.

Copy editing: Thierry Black
Proofreading: Didier Pilon
Typesetting: Édiscript enr.
Cover design: Lisa Marie Smith
Cover illustration: original design by Marie-Josée Morin, Les Éditions Sémaphore.

Library and Archives Canada Cataloguing in Publication
Poissant, Alain, 1951-
[Sort de Bonté III. English]
    The fate of Bonté III / Alain Poissant; translated by Rob Twiss.

(Literary translation collection)
Translation of: Le sort de Bonté III.
Includes bibliographical references.
Issued in print and electronic formats.
ISBN 978-0-7766-2285-9 (paperback).
ISBN 978-0-7766-2287-3 (pdf).
ISBN 978-0-7766-2286-6 (epub)

    I. Twiss, Rob, translator II. Title. III. Title: Sort de Bonté III. English IV. Series: Literary translation (Ottawa, Ont.)

PS8581.O237S6713 2015   C843'.54   C2015-907773-7
                                            C2015-907774-5

We acknowledge the financial support of the Government of Canada through the National Translation Program of Book Publishing, an initiative of the *Roadmap for Canada's Official Languages 2013-2018: Education, Immigration, Communities*, for our translation activities.

Printed in Canada.

A Second Portrait[1]

Alain Poissant grew up in Napierville, but he has denied that the story is autobiographical (Houdassine, 2014). Richard Boisvert (2014) called the novel "a love story that doesn't seem to be one."[2] Danielle Laurin (2013) wrote in *Le Devoir* that "The love story, if it exists, is barely grazed. And only at the end, at that. It's the journey, which never gives us the impression that it is a love story, that is fascinating." So if this novel isn't autobiographical fiction and it isn't really a love story, what is it? According to Ismaël Houdassine, "In the end, the novel is first and foremost a meditation on the passage of time and what it is that defines a place." And it's true: the author's home town seems to take on at least as much importance as any character in the story. Above all, Alain Poissant paints a portrait of Napierville.

Charles Le Blanc has noted the analogy between translation and portraiture:

> The portrait [...] is inspired by the nostalgic desire to memorialize one's own features or those of another. Its place in art is unique: whereas classical esthetics was based

---

1. I am grateful to professors Marc Charron and Luise von Flotow for their advice and support throughout this project.
2. Translations of Houdassine, Boisvert, and Laurin are my own.

on *mimesis*, the portrait, which also espouses imitation—
and thus involves faithfulness—is an imitation informed
by technique. It aims to immortalize beauty, but, as a cre-
ated object, relinquishes some of the attributes of nature
and takes on those of art. It is faithful, not to the subject
who sat for it, but to a *technique*, a way of seeing, an *intention*. […] A portrait can be faithful to the inner life of its
subject or to his social rank, which the artist intends to
emblematize. […] In some respects, a translation is to the
original as a portrait is to the subject who sat for it: a work
in which fidelity—whether to nature or to art, to Hermes
or to Apollo—is inescapable. (2012: 14)

Translators must decide, for the translation in general and
for each element of the translation, *what it is about the
source text they want to translate*. What, asks LeBlanc, is the
"*criterion* of truth?". By definition, the subject or source text
cannot be identical to the "intention" of the painter or
translator,[3] so there is an inherent conflict of interest in
both portraiture and translation. In both activities, it is necessary to mediate tension between fidelity to what you see in
front of you and fidelity to the ideal finished product you see
in your imagination.

Le Blanc observes another factor complicating translation: translators are "trapped" in language, constrained by
the semantic and aesthetic possibilities of words (11–12).
This observation can be assimilated into his portrait analogy.
A painter has a fixed number of paints, brushes, and tools
with which to complete the portrait. Anything she does must
be done with those resources, regardless of the similarity
between the colour of her paint and the colour of her subject's eyes, for example. When they are different, her techni-
cal ability may only take her so far. It is worth noting,
however, that her paint box may suggest certain brush

---

3. Minimally, because a person is not made of paint, and a translation is not writ-
    ten in the language of the original.

strokes or combinations of colours which appeal to the eye, regardless of their fidelity to the subject.

While I find Le Blanc's comments insightful and important, there are ways in which portraits and translations are different. First, the audience of a portrait is theoretically just as able to appreciate the subject as the portrait, but we normally read translations because the original texts are incomprehensible to us. In addition, the appearance of a portrait's subject is fixed by accidents of biology, while the portrait results from the deliberate application of paint; in contrast, both source text and translation are composed, deliberately, of words. The author is responsible for what he produces. As a result, the source text can be reverse-engineered to some extent. When reading a text, it is often possible to decide, rightly or wrongly, what the author was trying to achieve and how. Indeed, this "decision" is often an involuntary observation. Such reverse-engineering reveals that the author is also trapped in the system of language[4] and subject to certain, albeit less exacting, constraints of fidelity. Like the translator, the author is more or less restricted to a finite number of words with predetermined sounds and meanings, a limited number of paints and brushes. It might seem as if the author may be faithful to art alone, and not to nature, but this is not completely true. To the extent that Poissant aims at novelistic verisimilitude, he is beholden to, for example, speech patterns and cultural referents appropriate to his setting—certain features of his model.

That writing can be easily likened to painting is the reason that you probably did not find it odd when I wrote that "Alain Poissant paints a portrait of Napierville." But if my source text is a portrait, I need to adjust Le Blanc's metaphor to describe this translation. If Poissant's novel is a portrait of Napierville, this translation is a portrait of a portrait. Not a

---

4.   Le Blanc might object that the author is not as trapped as the translator. I would probably more or less agree with him, but I will not broach that subject here.

copy done for practice, but a second work of art done for a different audience and, crucially, with a different paint box.

I like this analogy, strained as it may be, because it materializes some of the variables; it provides a concrete way to think about what is possible and desirable in translation. For example, I might say that Poissant's portrait uses colours that I don't have. When Marquis' father, "the Welder," speaks to the priest about his son, Poissant marks his speech as that of a rural, blue-collar Quebecer by writing "Y" instead of "Il" (the standard French third-person pronoun). This vernacular is simply not available in written English, so one aspect of the source text—the accent—disappears from my translation. I'm not saying my hand was forced. I could have changed the spelling ("E" instead of "he," for example) to make the Welder speak English with a Quebec accent, or I could have even explicitly described his speech with an extra adverbial clause. But neither of those options was to my taste. I chose fidelity to my intention over fidelity to my subject when my tools wouldn't let me have it both ways.

It might also be that I have the same paint, but find that it combines differently with my other colours (Frawley 1984, 255–256). Towards the end of the narrative, Grazie remembers her childhood. She was young when her father lost his job; she never knew what he did, but she remembers him using English words like "grinder," "wrench," "floats," and "trucks" to describe his job. This overt notice that Grazie's father worked outside his community in his second language is significant in a novel where the relationship between vocation and identity is important for almost every character. It helps characterize Grazie in contrast to Francis, whose profession and identity were predetermined by his family. Ironically, using the same words in the translation blunts their impact, because they are surrounded by other English words. But no other acceptable choice presents itself. Here it is my very attempt to be faithful to the source that is responsible for the difference in the translation. The inverse shift occurs with proper names, such as the names of places, which

I have left in French: by reproducing certain features of my model, I turn what were relatively unremarkable structural details into explicit reminders of where the story is taking place.

Most of the time, of course, it's not so straightforward. Most of the time the tools and colours are similar, but not identical, and technique and creativity determine the extent to which I can balance the competing demands of fidelity to the source and fidelity to my intention. After Marquis' accident, someone asks him if he is hurt. One colloquial way to express concern in French ("ça va bien?") contains a non-literal use of the verb meaning "to go," a fact Poissant exploits for a clever paragraph-long play on words. Precisely the same trick is impossible in English, but other plays on words are not. You can decide for yourself what you think of my solution.

I am aware that it may seem odd, in a translator's fore-word, to draw attention to ways in which my translation differs from the original. None of this, however, should be read as an apology. It's true that some things are lost in translation, but Poissant's quirky, unromantic love story is good enough to be worth reading without them. And I have tried, within the bounds of my own creativity and highly subjective ideas of what constitutes good English prose, to preserve Poissant's dry humour and punchy, laconic style. I have tried, in short, to understand why this book is so enjoyable to read in French and to produce another that is equally enjoyable to read in English.

Rob Twiss

References

BOISVERT, Richard (2014). "*Le sort de Bonté III*: pendant ce temps à Napierville." *Le Soleil*. January 12. <http://www.lapresse.ca/le-soleil/arts-et-spectacles/livres/201401/11/01-4727828-le-sort-de-bonte-iii-pendant-ce-temps-a-napierville.php>

FRAWLEY, William (1984). "Prolegomenon to a Theory of Translation." In *Translation: Literary, Linguistic, and Philosophical Perspectives*. Newark: University of Delaware Press. 159–175.

HOUDASSINE, Ismaël (2014). "Une vache, un couple et Napierville: Alain Poissant, finaliste au Prix des libraires." *Le Huffington Post.* January 29. <http://quebec.huffingtonpost.ca/2014/01/29/alain-poissant-prix-des-libraires_n_4687883.html>

LAURIN, Danielle (2013). "Homme cherche femme, femme cherche homme." *Le Devoir.* May 25. <http://www.ledevoir.com/culture/livres/378903/homme-cherche-femme-femme-cherche-homme>

LE BLANC, Charles (2012). *The Hermes Complex: Philosophical reflections on translation.* B. Folkart (trans.). Ottawa: University of Ottawa Press.

A farm on a range. A model farm, like all farms in Quebec had become since the sixties. Vast fields that had been cleared of stones and drained deep. Lone trees standing against the horizon like knick-knacks on a shelf. Buildings covered in galvanized steel sheets gleaming in the sun. Black and white cows tied up in front of a trough all year long. Bony, cumbersome Holsteins often lame from lack of exercise and the unforgiving cement floors. Their horns had been burned off when they were very young, and the long strands of curly hair that now covered their scars made them look soft and disoriented, like stuffed animals. A wall of the milk room beside the stable was lined with photographs of breeding bulls. Beside each picture, a hurried hand had written the price of each pipet of semen, a price which, like everything in this world, obeyed the law of supply and demand. The inseminator would show up within six hours of the phone call with the semen preserved in a basin of liquid nitrogen. He would put on a long plastic glove that covered his entire arm and shoulder, and brush away the tail of the future mother. Bound by her collar or chain, she would raise her head for a second and arch her back as the groping hand sunk into her. This ultra-selective method of fertilization can, when breeders have an eye for the signs of ovulation, be just as successful as natural breeding. But life being what it is, the procedure did not always work. Animals that had calved several times already would suddenly appear to be sterile. These animals were called *anneillères*.

Bonté III was an *anneillère*. The inseminator had come several times, in vain. Month after month, the signs of ovulation returned. They were the same as with other animals— the swollen vulva, the discharge of clear mucus. She was ovulating, but no embryo would develop in her uterus.

Bonté III was five years old. At that age, a cow should be at her best. *Best* is an accounting term. A dairy farm is a business and must be run like one. From that point of view, the days of Bonté III were numbered. Numbered was not an empty word. She had represented her line very well. A cow does not have to try to be a cow. It simply lives a cow's life. The cycle is imposed. The cycle lends itself well to accounting operations. It eats. It drinks. It ruminates. It pisses. It shits. That all costs what it costs. It ovulates. It bears a calf. It gives birth. It produces milk. That all brings in what it brings in.

Francis raised cattle. Every morning and every evening he milked forty cows like Bonté III. He fed them and gave them water. He collected their manure and spread it in the fields. When necessary, he called the vet and purchased frozen sperm from the inseminator. He had done all this for Bonté III, as he had for her mother, Bonté II, and her grandmother, Bonté I, in exchange for their milk. Giving and giving. But the only thing to do now was to call the butcher.

Because it is what it is, thought Francis.

He stabbed his pitchfork into a bale of hay. He approached Bonté III and pushed the bale under her snout with a practiced gesture. They hay smelled good, like the green grass and dust of the prairies.

Unless…

He stabbed the pitchfork into another bale and moved on.

When all the cows had received their portion, Francis put down the pitchfork. He took a clean plastic bucket and filled it with water and powdered milk. The cows were coming in.

The breeding animals were kept in another part of the barn. Francis raised the bucket of diluted powdered milk to the mouth of the youngest. It had been born four days ago, and it was now time for it to be weaned off its mother's colostrum. Francis stuck his finger in the milk and then into the calf's mouth. The calf sucked off the milk, nudging in vain at an imaginary udder. Patiently, Francis pulled the calf's head down to the bucket. Drink! he said. Drink! The calf let go of his finger and raised its head. Its eyes were sad and empty. Sometimes it took a few days to change the instinct to suckle into the instinct to gulp down liquid. Drink! Drink, you idiot! Francis removed his finger and shoved the calf's mouth down into the bucket. The calf shook and mooed. They started again. When it had drunk down to the bottom of the bucket, its eyes became calm and warm.

It was a heifer. A male would have been sent away within hours of its birth to be fattened up for the butcher.

The other heifers were between a week and a month old. After a month, the calves would forget all about their mother's teats and be eating mash and dry hay like the other animals.

Francis turned off the lights but left the radio on full volume. Walking behind Bonté III, he looked at her vulva. Having her slaughtered would cost him. On both her mother's and her father's side, she came from a line of champions. Big, strong, healthy animals with almost perfectly white coats. Francis wouldn't go so far as to shout from the rooftops that he loved his cows, but he would brag about how well he took care of them. He was proud of Bonté III's milk yield, and a farmer's pride was a rare commodity.

But, he reminded himself, it is what it is.

The cigarette was already in his mouth, and he lit it the moment he got out the door. He had got up at five thirty, and the sun in the sky told him that it was around eight. His stomach rumbled. The cigarette made him feel pleasantly dizzy. He leaned against the wall. He continued to smoke and think about what to do with Bonté III while he inspected his clothes. A few wisps of hay or straw had stuck to his vest, but overall it seemed to him that his outfit was beyond reproach. After all, he worked in shit for hours at a time. Some days, he was up to his armpits in it, so to speak. Even after a long shower and a torrent of soap, he smelled. He smelled of cattle like he was one of the herd.

Beyond the river the sun was melting the last of the snow. Walking back to the house, Francis heard the first spring geese. A-honk. A-honk. A-honk. With one hand over his eyes, he looked up to find the V. It was moving north, like a single bird broken into pieces working together.

That's something, thought Francis. That's really something.

He watched them for a long time. Three times the bird at the head of the formation moved to the left and was replaced by the one behind. A-honk. A-honk. A-honk.

It's something, really something, to go to the other end of the continent just to fornicate and raise a brood.

Francis had never left his cows or his fields. He had never traveled. He had never slept anywhere but his own bed or on a bale of hay when a cow was giving birth or, sometimes, on the porch in the summer. When his father had died suddenly on his tractor at the age of thirty-nine, Francis had understood that he would not leave the farm. He borrowed his travels from migrating birds. He took his turn at the head of the flock. He pecked at the grass in the meadow. He stood guard with his neck straight up in the air. He slept with his head under his wing. He honked. He was a fictional character.

A-honk. A-honk. A-honk.

The flock slowly shrank and disappeared. Francis stood for a long time listening to them croak in the fresh morning air.

After scarfing down his breakfast, Francis smoked his second cigarette of the morning. He held it between his lips for a long while thinking about what would become of Bonté III.

All the cows were lying down when Francis went back to the stable. He walked over to Bonté III and made her get up. It is what it is, he said, benevolently. She was waiting for him to give her a handful of mash, and he did. She ate out of the palm of his hand and laid down again. Your reign is coming to an end, he said, walking away to call the butcher.

When the cows had left the barn, Francis lit his third cigarette.

He was walking towards the large shed when a flock of geese flew over the barn and landed on the side of the river. He watched them pecking around in the mud.

A farm was a continuous spectacle. There was the sky. There were cows. There were cats and dogs. There were geese. There were pigeons. There were sparrows. There were the farmers themselves, who, from the first nice days of spring, brought out their tractors and machines to display them beside their barns and sheds.

At noon, Francis went inside to eat. His mother greeted him as usual. They ate without speaking. Then Francis lit his fourth cigarette, standing beside the window. He would tell himself that the sky and the land were one. One face. One farce.

He lay down for a few minutes near the furnace vent on the living room floor and added a few figures in his head. Then he went out with his rain coat over his shoulder.

The sky and the land were still one. He washed his tractors and equipment with a pressure washer. While they were drying, he smoked a cigarette and looked at the sky and the land.

It was inevitable. When he looked out like that, he ended up asking himself questions. Questions that ceased to exist as soon as they had been asked, like the smoke from his cigarette.

How did the air and the stars in the sky become the kingdom of God? There had to be a history of God, an extraordinarily ordinary sequence of events. No person, no book had ever told him such a story. Didn't everything, no matter how large, no matter how insignificant, have a story? Even a cow had a story.

He had heard educated people say, on some radio station, that God was dead. They hadn't given the details. That didn't seem to be the point for them. Francis had not completely understood. But one question was bothering him. It was about death. He thought of the first men, stuck in their caves with the rotting corpse of a parent, a child, a friend. What to do? How do you get rid of a parent, a child, a friend, an immaterial link born in the heart that survived the decomposition of the flesh?

It was four o'clock when Francis finally saw the truck coming down the hill. He livened up and put out his cigarette. The driver slowed down and lowered the window. Francis, where is it? he asked. Francis pointed up to the buildings.

Here!

He led the truck to the barn door. The driver got out and lowered the loading ramp. Francis unhooked Bonté III. She followed him docilely. He climbed into the truck and she climbed in with him. He tied her up and gave her an affectionate pat. She turned her big frizzy head, and Francis saw a series of questions in her wide round eyes. The kind of questions you don't find on a quiz. Because it is what it is, he replied.

The next week, Francis had to work in the fields in addition to caring for the cows. Francis stopped the tractor. He felt dazed. He felt alone. In five days he hadn't slept much more than twenty hours.

The heat rippled on the horizon. The air was blue like the flame of a torch. There were mirages. Lots of them. Trees changed places. The sky shook the earth; the earth trembled.

When Francis turned the key and shut off the engine, a *fortissimo* silence fell on him. He closed and reopened his eyes several times. Hallucinations. People were walking there, in front of him, in the vibrating, whirling dust. Lots of people. Scores. Men and women and children. They pressed on like clouds pushed by the wind, with no other destination than the silence. Where did they come from?

He hadn't had anything to drink. He hadn't smoked anything. The people walked in a sort of unstable stream. They walked into each other. They split in two. But they didn't seem to move even one step forward. Stuck there, thought Francis. As if nothing good was waiting for them. As if they were not really dead, but almost. Had they been murdered?

Ghosts, that's the word, thought Francis, who blinked as he let himself get carried away with the illusion. How many were there? At least as many as there were leaves on that big linden tree over there. And packed just as tightly. He had never seen so many people in so little space. It was impossible to tell who was who. Faces. Arms. Legs. Stomachs. Breasts. Eyes that were far too big and ringed by huge dark circles. Francis asked himself what could be happening to make such a ghostly army invade the fields of Napierville. How long had it been since he'd watched the news or read the paper? He didn't get a minute to himself.

He thought of faraway lands recently ravaged by war, where he had never set foot. It was funny how Napierville had managed to escape the brutality of the world, other than for a brief period between 1837 and 1838. As far as the headlines were concerned, nothing violent had ever happened in Napierville. Absolutely nothing. Except that two people were hanged at the Pied-du-Courant in Montreal, and a dozen were exiled to Australia—their names were engraved on a stone in the middle of town, at the Pointe des Patriotes. It was a detail in history. A detail in geography. A void in the news. Although not much had been written about Napierville, there was a long history of the land's occupation. People had been living here for a long time. Those whom the colonizers, arriving by boat, had called the Damned Savages had probably cleared and cultivated a good part of North America in their own way before Europe had gotten its hands on the continent. Because the continent did not appear on the official maps of any European kingdom, the property rights of the Damned Savages in question had been null and void. Anyways, smallpox had cleared the land quickly enough, and had spared the costs of a military campaign in the process. No wars in Napierville. No genocide. No enemies. No tragedies. And no memory. None at all. The history books suggested 1837–1838 as the date of a possible popular uprising. But even that was not clear. The weapons and the banknotes had all wound up on the same side. The insurgents had failed decisively. Their idea of Lower Canada had been quickly squashed.

There had been no natural disasters either. No volcanoes. No hurricanes. No devastating earthquakes. Sometimes it rained too much. Sometimes, not enough. All in all, the farmers had been living off the land for two centuries. A little Eden, all of it. Just enough heat for two harvests of feed and grains. Just enough cold to feel it in your bones and quickly shut yourself inside to watch television or disappear to Florida.

Francis felt a sudden urge to have his say. He shook himself. The ghosts disappeared. There was no one there. The lost expanse of the fields. All that was left was him, the burning sky and the cultivated ground. He got down from the tractor and walked towards the rocky outcropping by the border ditch. This sometimes happened to him when he became too immersed in solitude: he was seized with a sudden desire to address the people of Napierville and, through them, all of humanity. The ghosts. The non-ghosts. Men. Women. Children. He summoned and addressed them all in the style of professional speechmakers.

History or no history, memory or no memory, Napierville or no Napierville, the problems to be solved were many. Everyone around here had their own personal ones, but you could get them down to just a few. It was feasible.

The very many poor people who wanted to be rid of the very few rich people.

The very few rich people who wanted to be rid of the very many poor people.

Hoarded wealth.

Obscure and non-obscure institutions through which the wealth moved.

First-rate, second-rate, third-rate moneylenders.

The internal rate of return.

Negative growth.

They were simple things, but they showed the extraordinary organizing power of money. Absolutely. Far more than the voting booth.

Francis climbed up on the mound. He felt scared. He took a last puff of his cigarette. He took off his cap. He looked into the distance and opened his arms wide. Let them say I'm crazy, he thought.

It was a first. Never before had someone given a speech from that mound. Citizens! he began.

His voice failed him. He'd barely made a sound. He started again. Citizens! Allow me to introduce myself. My name is Francis.

There, he had made his start. He had introduced himself. The void was filled. The silence overturned. He looked around him at the ground broken up by the harrows and farther away at the few groves that had not been cleared away by his ancestors.

Can you hear me? Can you hear me over there? In China? In Honolulu? In Conakry? In Atlanta? In Terrebonne? In Paris?

It was a first, that was certain. Something had been set in motion, something still vague, contorted, perhaps, but real. Was that not his own voice travelling so far? He had never spoken so loud. Not shouted, spoken. It gave him a thrill. All those absent people he addressed, those isolated people looking for company, those spectres reached by his words came together at a crossroads in the air like an extension of his self, of many other selves, a crowd.

Francis took a step forward. He straightened his neck. He fidgeted with his hands. It was strange how all of a sudden he felt out of breath and lost, completely lost on his own property. Speaking, speaking to a crowd, was not something just anyone could do, he supposed. Speaking at all was not something just anyone could do. A man in a field was never more than a man in a field. A man and a woman in a field were a couple. But now this was something that had never been seen before: a man on his own, a field, the whole world. It was the famous enigma of the tree falling in the forest when no one is around to hear it hit the ground. Except now the tree was a man, and he wasn't falling. He was speaking. The words flickered, then were carried away over the clumps of fresh earth. It was marvelous.

Francis stopped talking. He listened. He looked. The space had won. In the distance the wind was shaking the branches and turning over the leaves. Air currents blew up witches of dust. The weather was superb. It was one of those days the mind latches on to to make memories of happy times.

Visions passed through Francis' mind, one after the other. He saw himself as a child stretched out in the clover and the dandelions, looking up at the sky. A pleasant vision. He is wearing shorts. He has brought his two brothers with him. They are also stretched out in the clover and the dandelions. They are all snickering because the grass prickles their legs and their bare arms. They crush the clover and the dandelions in their hands to smell them. Sometimes they get up, they run, and they fall down and roll around in the grass like bears. Children amongst themselves. Another time. Francis didn't know about his brothers, but as far as he could tell, life didn't give you a ton of these visions. Unless you were an artist and could create your own with a paintbrush and colour. These were the visions that went way back, back beyond the reach of consciousness, but that, paradoxically, were the very substance and genesis of consciousness, like black strokes that, on a painting by a great artist, are light.

Francis looked all around. What was going on was what was usually going on in a field: nothing, nothing but the inevitability of the day and the seasons. The assembly summoned by a lone lunatic in a field had disappeared. No matter. There had never been a lunatic or an assembly. Only a man, alone.

There. I've said all I have to say. Thank you for listening.

He lowered his arms. He got back on his tractor. He started it up. It was strange how he felt tired, still tired. His hand was shaking. It was shaking far too much. Francis decided that the work in the field could wait. He got back off the tractor and detached the harrow. He got back on and returned to the house.

He went into his room and came out with a bunch of clean clothes. He undressed in the bathroom. He turned both taps all the way on in the shower. When the steam started to trickle down the mirror of the medicine cabinet, he got out of the shower, refreshed.

He put on a tie and a jacket. Upstairs, in a corner that had been converted into an office, he turned on the computer and set the camera on the windowsill.

It was unusual that a day in the fields ended with anything other than tiredness. Francis got the feeling that his life was falling into place. He imagined himself putting up notices on every post in town. A few months later, going into city hall with the woman who would move in, help him feed the calves in the barn, maybe even drive the tractor in the fields. He wouldn't be picky about the other details. It couldn't be worse than it was at that moment.

While the computer was coming online, he sat in front of the camera. He took five pictures. He uploaded them onto the computer, picked one, and wrote the ad.

5'9"
160 lb.
32 years old
Man seeks woman
Leave a message at the farm
Francis

In Napierville, the elementary school is in the middle of town, halfway between the Pointe des Patriotes and the arena. The principal, Aline, set her cup of coffee down on the cubby in the hall and unlocked the heavy doors to the schoolyard.

The first bus bringing children from the farms stopped beside the soccer field. The teachers' cars filed into the parking lot. The students dispersed and then reassembled. The oldest had brought their skateboards and barrelled into the yard, against the rules. The school year was coming to an end. No doubt they were dreaming of the holidays and acrobatics.

The bell told them to form lines. A squawking seagull from the wooded riverbanks vanished into the skeletal poplars.

The second bell sounded.

It was nine o'clock when the secretary, Margie, brought Aline the list of absences.

The same ones?

Yes and no. The Kid is absent for a third day now.

Aline asked Margie if she had called.

Yes. No one, as usual.

Three days in a row?

And last week as well.

Margie poured herself a cup of coffee and left the room. Later, she brought in the mail. Aline called the Kid's house herself. She let it ring ten times before hanging up.

Standing beside the window watching the other squawking seagulls out of the corner of her eye, she ran through the options that a school principal had when a student was repeatedly absent.

She could—solution number one—alert social services.

She could—solution number two—take care of it herself: visit the address, question the neighbours, talk to the mother.

She could—non-solution—do nothing.

The law said that school attendance was mandatory and that its enforcement was incumbent upon parents and teachers. Was the law perfect? Aline was in her thirty-eighth year of what was now called the teaching sector. Dogmatism had never been her strong suit. She thought of herself as an optimist. Things often worked themselves out. Other times they didn't.

The Kid stuttered. The other students made fun of him. He needed to see a speech therapist. The school didn't have one. The mother lived off small painting contracts and had no money.

Aline had met the Kid's mother at least a dozen times since September. There weren't many people like her. She was an independent woman who seemed to have taken it upon herself to make the people around her shed their usual avarice. She was special. But she wasn't stupid, far from it.

The Kid's mother was named Graziella. Eleven years ago she was still working at a bank in Montreal. She had been hired at seventeen. Less than a week had gone by when she was the victim of her first armed robbery. Two men, their faces distorted by nylon stockings, had come in raving like madmen. When they arrived at the counter, they didn't seem to know quite what to do, other than to wave what looked like greasy mechanic's tools in the air. A senior teller who had experience with this type of rapid transaction quickly emptied her till into a cloth bag and pushed the bag out in front of her. Behind her window, Grazie did the same thing. Satisfied, the two crooks left, brandishing their bags.

As always, after such incidents, which the bank directors and insurance companies called "workplace accidents," the victims had met with a shrink.

Waiting her turn in the hall—she was the most recent hire—Graziella calculated. She calculated the value of the theft. She calculated that ninety-nine times out of one hundred, the thieves were men. She calculated that ninety-nine times out of one hundred, the victims were women. She calculated that, behind the upholstered doors of the bank's offices, one hundred percent of the managers and directors of this and that were men. She calculated that the board members and the shareholders at the annual meetings were also men.

The shrink was a man. Grazie added that to her statistics.

But the shrink didn't want to talk about statistics. He wanted Grazie to tell him, now, in this moment, how she was feeling. She wanted her to tell him how she had felt when she saw the screaming masked armed men come in. What had she thought? Was she scared? On a scale of one to ten, how would she rate her fear? How had she reacted? How would she react the next time? Had she had nightmares? Was she worried she would? Again, right now, right here, how did she feel?

The questions didn't hurt, but Grazie didn't answer them. She told herself that she had been a victim of money, and that now she was a victim of psychology. A victim was better off saying nothing. You never know. Anyways, the shrink was talking. He suggested answers like a teacher talking to a student who had not learned the lesson. The words coming out of his mouth had nothing to do with money. The only thing Grazie wanted to say to the shrink was that the words he was saying were very, very confusing. Grazie suspected him of rearranging the facts.

In the confidential report to her employer, the shrink wrote that Graziella didn't seem to scare easily.

After a robbery, the bank let its employees go home a few hours early. Tomorrow was another day. Graziella would show up to work as usual.

A month passed before other robbers—or maybe the same ones—had barged in like wild men with their disguises and their weapons to scare the tellers, screaming: "Get your hands in the air! Get your hands in the air! Get your hands in the air!" Money, the great pacifier, had once again been put into the sacks and pushed out towards the robbers.

When the police—the same police—had left, the shrink—the same shrink—met with Graziella. He told her to sit in the same chair, asked the same questions, noted the same silence.

Required to submit an evaluation to his employer, the shrink had looked for a word that would sum up the young woman's attitude. He searched at length through typologies of mental illness. The problem with Graziella was that she was the archetypal teller. One of those young women between the ages of sixteen and twenty-five who had been filing in behind the counter ever since it had become more profitable for banks to employ women rather than men. Graziella liked bright red nails. She dressed well. She did her hair and makeup with just enough flair to catch the eye of the accounting clerks from among whom she would choose a husband while conforming to the neutral dress code the bank imposed on its employees. The men found her pretty.

And then? the shrink asked himself.

His training and experience told him that there had to be a fault behind the makeup and the clothes, but what was it? Unable to count on any spontaneous verbal utterance, he had opted for the usual search for indirect clues among small, significant details.

Her gaze. What was it about those pale blue eyes? Pride? Arrogance? Cold indifference? Surely not panic.

Her gestures. What did it mean when she tilted her head to the side like that when he addressed her? When she touched her hair when she entered the office? When she seemed to be chewing on nothing? Nothing. Nothing to confirm or disprove any state of mind whatsoever.

Her posture. Her head was always inclined to one side, to the right, like a cat deaf in one ear. Her legs crossed at the ankles: left in front of right. Her arm, her right arm, passed underneath her breasts, little pointed breasts on her sturdy torso, while her left arm, the elbow resting in the palm of her right hand, rose to support her chin. It was the pose of a person ready to get out of the chair and leave at any moment.

He liked to repeat the catch-all formula to himself: the devil is in the details. He continued his search. The little finger. The little finger of each hand. They seemed curiously long—longer than her ring fingers. A benign malformation, but, who knows, it could hide others. The great care she took to pull back the long hair on her neck into a bun held in place by a large flashy bronze comb. The heavy man's watch gaping around her wrist. The large brushed metal pendant in the shape of a heart hanging over her sternum.

At university, he had been taught that psychologists often made things up and told themselves stories. Ready-made ideas. Stories that fit.

Better off letting it go.

Which he did, writing in his report what he always wrote when he did not know what to say but had to have the last word: a person to watch.

While working at the bank five days a week, Grazie took night courses. Naturally, when she got her diploma in management, she applied to and joined the corporate loans department.

No one saw her around Napierville anymore. No one had heard any news. Was she married? Was someone supporting her? Did she have kids? It had been like this as long as cities had been creating wealth: the young people, those who did not have the luck or the opportunity to make their living in their own community, left their family and their friends, and no one heard of them until the day their name and photograph showed up on the last page of the newspaper. Then only a few old people remembered the young dreamers they had been.

In an anonymous, soundproofed office, Grazie pursued a career in the service of money, the kind of career a bank offered. She counted. She canvassed clients. She dressed with the utmost care. She did her makeup. She painted her nails. The men who saw her on the metro or dealt with her in her soundproofed office found her pretty, attractive. Every morning at ten to eight she took the elevator. At eight o'clock sharp she sat down behind a pile of folders and a mug of coffee. The minutes went by. The years went by. The bank's profits increased and were distributed among the shareholders and upper management.

Then one day, the delicate Grazie-money balance was upset. There had been no sign. No warning. Just a crisis. Why? What had happened that not even the sharpest financial analysts had been unable to foresee?

No one had seen her in three days. Charles from Security had been tasked with solving the mystery. He had called. He had left message after message. A month had passed. Meetings had been held. Comments about ingratitude and betrayal had been made. As were others, such as: You never know who you're dealing with. Depression? Deflation? Stagflation? Overwork? Fraud? Accounting audits had been conducted. Dismissal procedures had been commenced. Because banks don't admit defeat easily, the Security department had launched a full inquiry.

A few months earlier, the bank had accorded Grazie its special employee mortgage, and she had purchased a two-bedroom condo in a building that looked out over the Botanical Gardens. Charles from Security was trying to pick the lock when he was surprised by a man from the cable company. The man had called 911, and Charles had had to get out of there.

One of his colleagues returned a few days later. Before he picked the lock, he talked to all the neighbours. They all recognized her. They all said "hi" in the hallway. As for the last time she had been seen, no one was certain. She left in the morning. She came back in the evening. No one knew what she did with the time she didn't sell to the bank. A neighbour without a story. Most were surprised to hear that she had not shown up to work recently. The confusion and indifference of urban anonymity rather than a disappearance.

Charles' colleague had picked the lock without being interrupted. What he saw fit the image Grazie had presented at the bank. An impeccably clean apartment. Nothing left lying around. Kitchen things in the kitchen and bedroom things in the white-ash chest of drawers in the bedroom. Clean floors. Open magazines. Dirty laundry in the hamper, as if Grazie was still living in the apartment and had disappeared only from the world of money. But a sickly sweet odour of rotting fruit indicated that the trash had not been emptied for some time. In the living room, on the little table by the window, was a bouquet of wilted flowers. Photographs broke up the white neutrality of the walls and showed that there was a family somewhere. There were also two paintings, real ones, showing that Grazie liked to go to art galleries. The inspector leaned in to read the names of the artists and concluded that, though Grazie had enough money to have paintings on the walls, she did not have enough money to have names on the paintings.

The only indication of any social life whatsoever were condoms in their wrappers and a box of condoms in the drawer in the bedside table. Strange, strange, thought the inspector: if you wanted to disappear to live another life, wouldn't those be the first thing you thought to bring with you? In the closet hung clothes on hooks—suits, little dresses, vests, coats.

When he got back to his desk, the inspector sifted through the last few months of transactions in her checking account and her savings account. Grazie spent what she earned. Nothing but preauthorized payments.

Faced with such an impasse, the inspector had contacted the local police station. A meeting had been held with the office of missing persons. A file had been opened and a description forwarded to the patrol officers and morgue employees. It was only a search on paper. People still had the right to disappear. At least, it wasn't against the law. As for the condo that looked out over the botanical gardens, the law gave the bank the right to repossess it.

The people of Napierville didn't know about any of this. As far as they were concerned, Graziella was simply back after an absence of several years. A new Graziella, but a recognizable one. Where were you? they had asked.

Summer had just begun. Thankfully. Because it was clear that Grazie was now sleeping outdoors on public benches. In Napierville, you didn't have to fight for the public benches. There were only a few of them, in front of the monument at the Pointe des Patriotes. Other than their ghosts, no one had spent the night there before.

But an absence of several years did not explain her homelessness or the other changes. Grazie no longer wore her hair in a bun. She no longer wore lipstick, eyeliner, nail polish. Two weeks after she arrived, she had not changed her jeans or her shirt. Shocking. It made no sense.

There must have been a disaster. Something no one had heard about and from which Grazie had had to flee.

When she wasn't sleeping, she begged. You didn't have to fight over spots to beg, ether. The only place busy enough to panhandle was in the middle of town, between the bank, the Métro grocery store, the building-materials store, and the post office.

A month had passed. Graziella's family had done what they had to. The CLSC had done what it had to. The SQ had, as well. But the Graziella who had returned to them was not the hardworking student they remembered. She did not want to hear about it. She didn't want to hear about anything. She was clear: don't bother me.

But she did not seem disturbed or depressed. She made no negative or defeatist or suicidal comments. No swear words. No soliloquies. No alcohol. No drugs. She seemed like someone who, while living with other people, refused to be like other people and demanded a place for herself.

When she had enough money to eat, she left her bench at the Pointe des Patriotes and went to the restaurant, Chez Gilles. Gilles let her sit at the back, behind the newspaper display, and served her the special. She ate and then stayed to read the newspaper or listen to the conversations. Not a word. Or, if she spoke, it was with her mouth closed.

As fall approached, she started going to the restaurant even when she didn't have any money for coffee or the special. Gilles served her a reheated poutine and tea. When he asked her to leave, she left.

They got along rather well. He felt he understood her. It's personal, he told his wife, Jacinthe; it's a bad connection between her and herself. He used his heart to understand the situation; his wife pouted and used her head, a missing piece of the puzzle.

Gilles thought there might have been a love story. Nothing was harder to rectify than a love story. Love, banal or fantastic, was on everyone's lips and in everyone's lives. What could be more precarious, more easily destroyed?

Graziella and he were the same age. He had known her at school as a child. He had watched her grow into a good-looking woman. At the age of six she'd already had those alluring eyes. That beautiful blond hair, too. For Gilles, Grazie was one of the very many young women in and around Napierville he could have married. Circumstances had dictated that Jacinthe was in a certain place at a certain time and that a one-night affair had lasted for fifteen years. A love story. Gilles got the impression that Grazie had not got what she deserved. Fate had fucked up. Fate had that power— the power to fuck up the dreams of even the most intrepid people.

The brief period of warm weather in Canada was over. School, work, and television made up families' lives. The maple leaves were changing colour. The days were getting shorter. Soon there would be a frost and the public benches would become intolerable. Again, Graziella's family did what needed to be done. So did the CLSC. So did the SQ. Grazie didn't want anything to do with it.

Then Gilles and his wife realized that they hadn't seen Grazie in... in how long? She was repeating her disappearing act from the bank in Napierville. A week went by. Then a month.

People at the restaurant talked about nothing but the cold and hockey. The municipal employees were told to hang Christmas garlands along the streets and at the Pointe des Patriotes. The businesses followed suit. Gilles put up a snowman and plastic candles in the window of his restaurant. To keep up the momentum, he started serving turkey on his dinner menu.

One day he made fusilli. His wife, Jacinthe, had served the customers who were in a hurry and then slipped away: she had to visit her mother who was battling lung cancer. Gilles filled the plates and brought them to the tables himself. A couple had just sat down at table six and were watching the falling snow through the window. Gilles thought to himself that he had seen that pretty woman before. Busy and distracted behind the flapping kitchen doors, Gilles had not paid attention when she had come in. It was Grazie. A Grazie who was pretending not to recognize him. A different Grazie from the one who kept to herself. A radiant Grazie.

A year had passed. Gilles could have predicted what would happen. He knew Marquis. He knew him better than he knew Graziella, or even his own wife, Jacinthe, by virtue of that primitive affinity between men. Marquis was special. He knew what he was doing around women. He was good with them. Few men loved them as much. He was sentimental. Immediately so. After only a few months, his eyes would begin to wander, and he would not wander back.

The principal entered, followed by the Kid. The class had split into little groups that talked loudly with their backs to the door. The Kid walked into the noise. He set his backpack down on his desk and took off his jacket. Underneath, he was wearing a red t-shirt with white trim, on the back of which was the name and number of a hockey player. The principal whispered something to the teacher, and the teacher whispered something to the Kid. The Kid took off his cap and stuffed it under his desk.

The school had adopted the rosy methods devised by the pedagogues at the Ministère de l'Éducation. The students obtained their diploma the same way they played, grew up, and watched television: without realizing they were doing it.

The day's lesson was on the capricious rules of agreement for past participles. This lesson was first taught in grade three and would return every year until the students left for university. Each group received a copy of a text containing eighteen participles; their task was to read each sentence and fish out the eighteen verb forms in question.

The principal left, and the Kid quickly put his cap back on. He looked around and then took it off again. There were still specks of paint on the backs of his hands and on his arms.

The teacher bent down to her student's level. How is it going? she asked. The Kid didn't know if he should answer. He pouted sullenly and emptied his backpack by flipping it upside down. He then kicked the contents under his desk. When he saw his cap, he bent down and put it back on his head again.

The teacher brought her face near the Kid's. She smiled, but it was a forced smile that showed she was in no mood for laughter. Take off your cap, she said. Everyone else takes their caps off in class. The Kid fidgeted and screwed his face up. Take it off, repeated the teacher. The Kid refused. The teacher gave the visor a flick. Off fell the cap.

The teacher regretted it immediately. Too often these days she lost her patience. And too often she did not know what to say or what to do to get her students to listen. Teaching had turned out to be a thousand times harder than she'd imagined it would be, based on her happy time as a student. She was spent. She didn't like who she was. At the end of the day, she was empty. Totally unmotivated. She would get home and ask herself: when exactly does the exhaustion begin? She looked at herself in the mirror, and another face looked back at her. There were now two short wrinkles over her nose and another running across her forehead: the wrinkles of an underappreciated, underpaid employee.

The Kid picked up his cap and put it back on without paying her any attention. He half closed his eyes and stiffened his neck. It was as if he was testing the teacher's ability to formulate, analyze, and solve the problem.

To her great surprise, he took a deep breath, took off his cap, and rejoined his group.

Then the bell went brrrring. The Kid took his time as the class poured into the hall. He put his pencil away in his pencil case. He put the pencil case away in his desk. He put his French booklet with the other booklets and the grammar textbook with the other textbooks.

Zip! He closed up his backpack. The teacher was wiping off the board. She turned around. What was the Kid waiting for?

He ate alone in the cafeteria. Outside, two teams had formed and gotten hold of a ball. Lines had been drawn on the pavement. The game was to throw the ball as hard as possible at the other team. It was an exceptionally social and aggressive game. The kind for which the Kid showed even less aptitude than he did for talking.

The hot sun made him want to sleep. He shook himself and kept walking. The monitor had her back turned, so he went back to the classroom.

The teacher was eating at her desk. When the Kid came in, she shut her eyes. He walked to her desk. He opened his backpack. He looked inside for a while, then shrugged his shoulders. Do you need something? asked the teacher. Yy-yess. What? I-I d-d-don't know…

Better to not push the subject.

She smiled at him to make him more comfortable. He approached. He touched her hand softly. Then he kissed her on the mouth. She forced herself not to yell. She forced herself not to smack him. I-I'm s-s-soorrry…

Several dozen posters had been put up here and there in town. Man seeks woman. Graziella had taken one down and put it in her bag, thinking: woman seeks man.

Up on a stepladder with her paintbrush, she wondered who was this guy named Francis. Napierville wasn't that big. She had surely seen him at some point: blond hair, small eyes, shirt collar open with a messy tie, looking like he had spent the night on a clothesline.

Outside a bird was singing. C-c-can you h-hear it? asked the Kid, who refused to go back to school. I hear it, said Graziela. Wh-wh-what's it c-called? I wish I knew, but I don't. D-d-d, d-d-d. She realized that he wanted a word, any word, as if for him words were containers that you could fill with wonderful things, like treasure chests. Come with me, said Graziella.

They went out through the French doors onto the front steps. In just a few days, the May sun had restored the trees to their magnificence. The brand new leaves glinted like petals in the sunlight.

The chirping of the bird without a name was getting more and more elaborate. Wh-wh-wheeere i-is it? Somewhere over there. Graziella pointed towards the foliage of a box elder. Wh-wheeere? Look!

Without waiting, the Kid jumped down from the steps and moved out onto the muddy ground. Don't scare him, whispered Grazie. The Kid slowed down. Then he crouched down low on all fours, imitating a cat. In the shelter of the leaves, the bird continued singing.

The Kid wondered whether it was really the same bird that they had been hearing since they started painting this new house. He stopped to inspect each part of the foliage. His mother had said that the bird in question was so small that he could hold it in his hand. Tiny. The problem was finding it. What colour was it?

Talking to himself with his mouth closed, the Kid slowly circled the tree. He encroached upon the shimmering freshly cut grass of the neighbouring property. His mother let him be. She would have liked to be able to teach her child the name of this stranger who had been entertaining them while they worked over the past three days. She knew the names of birds that lived deep in the jungle—toucans, parakeets, macaws—but not the name of the one singing above her head. She would also have liked to teach him what the bird was singing about. Because it had to be singing about something. A kind of story with rhymes, refrains, and declarations. For whom? Why was she so ignorant? Not just her, but the people around her, too. She had heard the same chirping as a child, and no one had been able to explain to her why a bird would sit alone way up in a tree to tell a bird story with such enthusiasm.

The Kid had gotten up and was now walking around the tree, picking his boots up high over the soft, full spring grass.

A door closed. Slam. A voice travelled through the air. A shout. Get away! Go home! The Kid was so shocked that he stayed where he was, his heart pounding and his feet paralyzed. It was a loud, fat-woman's voice. Fuck off! He felt like the tree was going to fall on him. Part of him continued to look for the bird in the leaves. Part of him thought he saw a tuft of wild feathers glide past a branch. Part of him panicked completely. He tripped. He crawled on his elbows, he got up again. Part of him let out a final sigh of relief. His mother wasn't scared of anyone. If a fat woman with a big voice had a problem with her, she would confront her.

Once he had reached the safety of the front steps, the Kid turned around. His mother was walking forward. The Kid imagined pleasantly that the tree was also moving forward and that the fat woman had no chance of escaping her thrashing.

As it happened, however, the fat woman wasn't scared of anyone, either. They were trading insults. As though watching a pantomime, the Kid got the message. He waited for it to end. I wonder where she learned all that, he asked himself. His mother didn't know much about singing birds, but she knew how to shout. As for the fat woman, she didn't give any ground. The Kid got the feeling that the two women knew each other. There had no doubt been a time when the fat woman had not been fat and when his mother was not yet his mother. Napierville had a fertile history, and no doubt its inhabitants descended more or less directly from a handful of foul-mouthed founders.

As with all such fights, a difficult silence followed the last words. Apparently the fat woman had no voice left, and his mother, no words.

Later, the Kid asked what was the name of the fat woman with the loud voice. The bird had not come back. They had gone back to work. Grazie stopped painting her part of the wall and looked at her son. What is it you want to know, exactly? The Kid continued painting in his corner. Despite his age, he could easily handle a large, full paintbrush. After he dipped it in the bucket, he would turn it once and wipe it

on the rim. He applied the paint in one downward movement, then evened it out with light strokes. Her name is
Marielle, said Graziella. Y-y-you kn-know her? Yes and no,
said his mother. She looked tired, fed up. It was in the tone
of her voice. Yes and no was often the kind of answer the Kid
got when she was fed up with questions and kept the answers
for herself.

He was also fed up and he didn't insist. Since the morning they had been painting a freshly built house that still
smelt like plaster. They had started by cleaning up the dust
from the sanding. Then they had set up the canvas sheets.
They had taped over some of the moulding and removed the
rest. They were applying the base coat. When they had
painted the other coats, they would varnish the doors and the
moulding. The contractor, Phil Fournier, had promised them
a bonus if they finished within five days.

At noon, they stopped and ate their Cheez Whiz and
ham sandwiches. Two other houses were being built down
the road, and the permits had been granted for a third. And
on the other side of town, a great big sign attached to tempo-
rary scaffolding announced a new development in anglicized
French: *Napierville Phase II*. Phase III was still inside the
head of the developer, Sam Samson. He was going to knock
down what he called a few old cabins and build new ones in
their place. The town would be unrecognizable.

Grazie lived in one of the old cabins scheduled for demo-
lition. She hoped she would get that bonus. She especially
hoped she could convince the municipal council and Sam
Samson not to knock down her house. He was from this
place and so was she. He had a reputation as a miser and only
paid once the job was done. With a cheque she would have
to take to the bank.

After he ate, the Kid fell asleep on the canvas. In spite of
the strong latex smell, Grazie closed the windows so that he
would sleep for a long time. She wanted a cigarette. She often
suddenly wanted a cigarette. She had also quit because,
bizarrely, she'd suddenly wanted to. She hadn't lapsed.

Tobacco was a drug. As for the cravings, they seemed to want to stay for life, tormenting her like a thorn in her side.

Now the Kid was snoring. Grazie looked at him with concerned tenderness. He wasn't small anymore, or young. There was nothing for it: he was growing, and, as he grew, he looked more and more like his father, Marquis. Nothing for it. He had that heap of dark black hair and those strong, powerful features that she had found so attractive. Nothing for it. Except that he stuttered. Questions. Answers. Like there was a knot in his throat that strangled the words one by one. Like the gears were broken.

She got back to work. The Kid woke up after an hour and started to cry. He still often cried when he woke up, without being able to stop. Choking on spasms of sadness. He hid his face.

When he was a baby, Graziella had held him almost constantly. And then he hadn't wanted to be held. Something had happened in his head. He cried alone in his corner until he was exhausted. She had talked to the doctor. He had told her not to worry; the tears didn't mean anything.

She worried anyways. No one liked to see tears. No one liked to see a child struggle alone in his corner against the whole world. Grazie was scared for him. A heavy, paralyzing fear. The distress of children was not that of adults. Grazie saw how he shut his eyes. She saw how he hiccupped. She heard the way he read. She saw the way he huddled and folded in on himself, a prisoner in his own head.

She put down her paintbrush. She went over to him. She sat down and hid her own face behind her knees and her hands. She shut her eyes so tight it made her dizzy. A mother could do that: enter into the world of her child and reattach the threads. She stopped seeing. She stopped hearing. She was submerged in an ocean of sadness. Swell. Wind. Wet. Devastation. Misery. Uncountable deaths that had nothing to do with Napierville but that still made her tremble.

The Kid's breathing became easier. He stopped trembling. She guessed that he was wiping his eyes on the sleeves of his sweatshirt. She heard him sniffle loudly. She gave him a tissue. When they both had dry eyes and noses, they got back to work.

4

The dog was running as fast as it could diagonally towards the road. The yellow school bus was going as fast as it could, too. The dog was in trouble. The yellow school bus was going much faster than the dog was.

Marquis was driving. Mechanically and without concern he navigated the road's curves and ordinary dangers. He saw the big dog at the last second. By last second, he meant that his eye, as he would later tell the police officers who came to take his statement, had registered barely two or three hazy images of what happened. One instant, there was nothing but the road, the next, the dog and the bus were where they never should have been. The questions of what to do and how to do it had never been asked for the simple reason that from the start it had been too late for questions.

Marquis had been driving since he was eight years old, in other words: forever. That was what saved him from rolling the bus, which was happily free of students this late in the morning. Thousands of hours driving tractors, trucks, and cars had sharpened his senses and coordinated his movement to the highest degree. Like an artist he had hit the brakes and steered the vehicle to the left. A reflex.

Then a few things happened all at the same time. Things that came from all directions at once, like a runaway story. The dog was thrown to the side of the road. The bus stopped half in the ditch, half on top of the chain-link fence. He heard car horns. His right hand shut off the engine. An obsession seized Marquis' mind: smash open the windshield and run through the fields. But lightning shot through his chest and his muscles refused to obey. An unusual weakness took hold of him. An accident, he thought.

He was sad about what had just happened. All his colleagues considered him a good driver. Maybe better than good. In forty years of roaming from one side of Quebec to the other, he had never caused an accident. Just one fender-bender, on a Sunday afternoon in Montreal, when a car had crossed two lanes to turn in front of him without signaling.

Other people he knew liked to drive. They were, as they say, happy behind the wheel. They felt that moving around at high speeds was something you could be proud of. There was a road inside them. They drove. Not him. He didn't hate it. Driving, for him, was just something he had always been able to do. Like all the sons of farmers and craftsmen at the time, he had driven his first vehicle, a pick-up, as soon as he was big enough to reach the pedals and shift gears at the same time. Driving a school bus was easy, except that he had to do it twice a day and five days a week with the students squabbling in his ears.

Marquis heard an unpleasant sound. Someone was frantically knocking on the folding door of the bus. The noise made him realize how nervous and agitated he was. Marquis thought that you could be afraid without having a reason to be afraid. A treacherous fear. At the same time, he told himself that he was confusing fear and surprise. He had only hit a dog and gotten mixed up. Fear couldn't get in through such a small opening. Unless fear was always there between your ears and had in a way neither beginning nor end. It was a cartridge in the chamber of a gun and, in the right circumstances, a bang happened.

A bang had happened, and Marquis felt that some time would pass before the scattered parts of him fell back into place. His breath. His sight. His heart. His head. His ass.

He had trouble breathing.

He had tunnel vision.

His head weighed a ton.

And that was not all. He felt a pain radiating from his left shoulder and arm. He felt his torso contract.

People were still yelling and banging at the door. People Marquis didn't know from Adam. They were gesturing. They wanted to know if he was doing ok.

The verb "to do" applied to the vitality of an "I" had always perplexed him. How are you doing? He was incapacitated. His internal compass was shaken up. What are you doing when you are "doing ok" or "not doing ok"? There should be a specific word, or a few. Brief sounds, monosyllables that, said at the right moment, would confuse no one. A clear message. No bullshit. A clear code. But who knows? Maybe there was a reason for such a linguistic mess. One or several reasons that had to do with living together. With gregariousness. With the pleasure of agreeing to talk about good and evil, black and white, sunny and dark, without stumbling into ethics. How are you doing? Which route did you take? Where did you come from? Where are you going? Only one possible response—the reply, the repetition: how's it going? An exchange.

While awaiting linguistic reform, Marquis was ready to admit that, if there was someone who was doing ok, who had always been doing ok, it was him. Even at that moment. He smiled. Smiling could only reassure the pests who were shouting and banging on the door of the bus. At the same time, if there was someone who was not doing ok at that moment, it was also him. Really not ok. He tried to get out of his seat, but could not. Don't you look great, he thought. Just great.

The collision between the dog and the school bus had happened near the forest the locals called the Bois à chevreuils for the deer that lived there. Marquis had often seen them in January and February, when the kids went back to school and the days were still short. They were cute animals, and he had a hard time imagining them being hunted by well-fed humans who couldn't help but kill them. They were animals with thin coats, and he had a hard time imagining them enduring -25° winter nights. They were animals that could hardly still be called wild, as they lived off of crops grown for cattle. Ruminants. And how! They could live for a long time digesting tree bark. Marquis liked ruminants. He had grown up around calves and cows. When he was eight years old he began working hard to take care of calves and cows in his grandfather's stable. Now that the buds were opening and the woods would soon again be filled with soft leaves, you wouldn't see the graceful little animals bent down at the edge of a field, quickly raising their heads with their mouths full of corn leaves the colour of packing tape. They would have lots to eat in the bush and would hide until the end of fall.

They—the inquisitive people who had gotten out of their cars—were pushing hard on the door. What's the rush?! Marquis wanted to yell that there was no fire. What had just happened was only a minor accident. A dead dog, dented metal, wasted time. When he felt like he could breathe again and his heart settled down, Marquis would pull on the lever that opened the doors. Let's say in a few more seconds.

He looked at the faces through the narrow windows. They looked close and far away at the same time. They were all turned towards him. They all babbled. They all looked at him accusingly. Like a jury gone mad. What had he done? Nothing. He had even prevented the worst from happening. It was just a dead dog. It was a close call. A figure of speech, but also an alarming reality. Everything felt close. He was suffocating. Sweat covered his forehead and temples. He felt the drops get heavier. At the same time, he was shivering. The cold heat of a sick man. He was numb.

Slowly, arduously, Marquis lifted his large body. He turned. The people were pressing their faces against the glass of the door and seemed to be hollering. He looked in the rear-view mirror. He looked for the car he had narrowly avoided after hitting the dog. Surprise: it was not just one car, but a whole line that stretched out behind his bus.

Marquis sat back down. He felt hot. He felt cold. He felt bad. Maybe he was even hallucinating. On top of the car horns and the pounding of his heart, he thought he could hear the screaming siren of a police car. His head and his chest became an echo chamber. It was at that moment that Marquis noticed a presence behind him, between the benches. Someone was running up the aisle.

Are you doing ok? the person yelled.

Marquis had a problem. A huge problem, the nature and extent of which were lost on him. Or maybe a series of little problems that came together to form an overwhelming constellation. His malaise endured. His shaken consciousness could distinguish between before and after, but he could not yet string together recent events. From his position, lying down, he could see no solution. Maybe there was none. From this helplessness came a feeling of defeat, of cowardice.

Several hours had passed. Inquisitive people had asked him questions. Police. Paramedics. Nurses. Doctors. So far he had said that he was doing fine.

Then someone had visited him. Who? He couldn't remember. They had joked around. About what? He couldn't remember that either.

It was now the middle of the night. He was lying on his back. The narrowness of the bed was part of the problem, but there was something more.

In the bed beside him someone was gasping. A man? A woman? He tried to listen. A throaty gasp that opened wide then shrunk down to nothing. That man or woman was desperately trying to breathe. A mountain of effort for a few molecules of oxygen. It smelled like the bitter sweat of exhaustion.

Then the wheezing stopped and the room was plunged into absolute silence, like at the end of a concert. Marquis turned his head. Something immense was coming. Or was he going? What was it? Where did it come from? It was as if he saw flashes of lightning that disappeared instantly into a dark night. A faraway storm. Marquis raised himself up on his elbows and straightened his neck. He hurt. He hurt a lot. Pain so well grafted onto his body was not about to go away. But there was something else. What was that swaying that was churning his stomach and made his head spin so much? Marquis was terrified of falling. Even the height of the bed bothered him. When he was a child, he had trained himself to walk on a beam in the barn. His older brother had promised to show him how not to be afraid. Show was maybe not the right world. Once at the fair his older brother had seen a tightrope walker do somersaults on a beam no wider than a hand. He had seen it—seen it with his own eyes—and convinced Marquis that they would become famous millionaires by doing somersaults on a beam. They would learn. The beam in the barn was thirty feet long. It was halfway up the wall of the building. Marquis climbed up the ladder. His brother looked up at him from below. To test him, his brother had said that someone had to stay on the ground to pick up the pieces. Marquis got up and looked at the other end of the beam. Thirty feet in the air, it looked as narrow as a matchstick. His older brother told him that he just had to try until he figured out the trick. There had to be a trick. Like riding a bike. Once you learned the trick, you never forgot. One step at a time. One foot in front of the other. Eyes on the holes. He wasn't shaking. He held up his own weight and the weight of the world with it.

At that moment, Marquis felt like he was on the beam, more unsettled than ever. Step by step, he walked forward.

He opened his mouth. His heart was beating. The adrenaline was heating his veins. Alive. He felt alive, but with an open grave below him as he walked.

In the barn, Marquis had decided that an older brother was never really a brother. He had better figure out the trick on his own.

But there was something more than the vertigo. Something was wrong with time. It was slowing down. It was coming apart. It stopped moving forward. As if the spool had run out. Marquis saw the dark end of his life. It occurred to him that the dark is never really the dark—just like silence is never really silence. So many things were shining there, on that dark surface, like fireflies. Marquis was surprised, surprised to learn something about himself: he had loved life.

The stupid love of a young child.

All those women he had loved, starting with his mother. What luck to all of a sudden see them all together again. His sister. The young girls at the school where he had learned much more than reading and counting. Their beauty enthralled. Their beauty radiated. The collection of petals that were the folds of a skirt on the thighs. The smell of their hair when he kissed them on the neck and they ran away giggling. Their delicate eyelids. Their round arms. Each brick of the building gave off its magic. After the village school, it had been the polyvalente. Marquis was more enchanted than ever. Harpooned. The years had changed nothing. He had in a sense married the little group of women in Napierville and the surrounding areas. He had let himself go. Roads, streets, houses; a wandering love. Watching. Approaching. A few words. A few caresses. Embraces. Names and family names started to come back to him. Affectionate pet names. Restaurant tables. Grocery-store aisles. The church. The town hall. The bank.

The small child had never become an adult. He had stayed where he had come from. He had lived his life in the village, married to Napierville. Why would he have led any existence other than his own and that of the women of Napierville? Napierville may be a small town, but it is home to a multitude. Montreal and New York were just as present in the minds of its residents as they were in the minds of Montrealers and New Yorkers.

Today the child was incarnated in its final avatar. Death was doing a great job. Marquis understood that they would come with him. The little girls and women of Napierville. The tour of wonder was over for him. The dust and the shadows opened up to him with arms that had nothing feminine about them.

He was leaving Napierville. His heart had first given out a few hours earlier in the yellow school bus. Now it was giving out for good. That was the sum and substance of the problem. His heart. It was derisively called the ticker. His ticker had given out. A small, vigilant muscle that mostly went unnoticed. A barely discernable pulse in the carotid artery and the wrists. The sound of the waves amplified when the cone of the ear was glued against the pillow.

For handy doctors, it was a pump. They opened up the rib cage. They attached a machine. They grafted in the muscle of a corpse. Then they finished the job with an electric discharge. Life returned.

For believers, it was the receptacle of the soul. The source of goodness. The source of prayer. It was by the heart that you were sanctified.

For moralists, it was the symbolic crucible of good and evil.

For poets, it was the barometer of love.

Marquis felt a swelling within himself. Barely a distraction. Like he was falling. Falling outside of the limits of this world. To the other side. He shivered. Already he felt better.

All the alarms of the monitoring devices at the head of the bed went off at the same time. The room filled with concerned faces and busy hands.

The last thought of the dying ran through Marquis' head: would a version of himself persist in the sky above Napierville?

Like a period of overtime in hockey? He had listened to so many platitudes about life after death that he had to ask himself if he wasn't already there.

5

Fate had been testing Marquis' family for several years. As though the sky above Napierville conspired against them.

Fate had struck first when Marquis' father was sent to prison. He was sentenced to two years less a day for tax fraud. Of those two years less a day, the man everyone in Napierville called the Welder had served one sixth. Thus was the law of conditional releases. The criminal had to express regret, of course. He had to represent a low risk for society and zero chance of reoffending. Finally, he had to put aside the idea that money earned through work is personal property, and adopt a quasi-religious devotion to the redistribution of wealth, even if he did not give a damn for religion. Society giveth, society taketh away; he was not a believer.

At the time, Marquis' father was fifty-eight years old. He was a man who did not let himself be pushed around. He had always been a man who did not let himself be pushed around, and the four months in prison did nothing to soften his abrasive personality.

Once released he returned to the head of the welding business that he had spent thirty years building and that his tax problems had brought to the brink of failure.

Had he thought that his clients would stay faithful? Clients from Napierville, but also from the surrounding towns and villages. Clients he had served well and who had always been satisfied. Could he not make anything that could be made out of iron? Had he not watched his uncle working with a blowtorch before putting the helmet on himself and welding his first seam at the age of twelve?

At one time the company had employed twelve welders. It now employed only one: its founder and sole owner, now up to his ears in debt.

Fate had struck again with the death of the Welder's eldest son. Death as a kind of condemnation, taking someone still young and beautiful with a successful professional life.

The eldest son's name was Jean-Jacques. He was homosexual. He had always been homosexual. At least since he was twelve years old. He had been actively homosexual for eight years at the Catholic boarding school, and then at McGill University where he had studied medicine. AIDS appeared a few years later. It appeared and the panic spread as it had spread during the great epidemics of centuries past.

Jean-Jacques had just turned thirty-five. Like everyone in his family, he was exceptionally strong and broadly built, with the hands and shoulders of his blacksmith and farmer ancestors. In less than three short years, opportunist infections made him unrecognizable. Skin and bones.

Occasionally, a disease will make heroes, and the heroes will give courage to those who need it. AIDS didn't make any heroes. Jean-Jacques died in quarantine in a room of the same hospital where he used to save lives. His family only found out a week later from an employee of the morgue.

The third blow came soon after. The neighbours heard an explosion. On their front steps, they watched the flames lick the contours of the windows of the welding shop.

They ran. At the back of the workshop, the flames were already going out. A man lay on the ground next to the folding door. The exploding gas reservoir had thrown him twenty feet. The Welder—it had to be him—had burns on his face and hands. They drove him to the hospital where he was treated quickly at the burn unit. He survived and even returned to his work. But along with the skin of his face, the explosion had taken the last of the man's good humour.

The new priest in Napierville—the parishes of the diocese had a high turnover rate for priests between the ages of sixty and eighty—had never seen a face so cruelly devastated by scars. He pretended not to notice and warmly invited the Welder to come in.

The vestibule opened directly onto the great dining hall that had, at a time when French-Canadian Catholicism prospered, held up to forty guests at the same table. The walls were decorated with framed photos of popes, bishops, and vicars arrayed in their priestly vestments and distinctions.

The immense table served as a desk, and metal filing cabinets, like those in any administrative office, had replaced the buffets and cabinets that once held dishes and tablecloths.

The priest asked his guest to sit down. The smooth shine of burnt skin was tempered by the dim light. The man was well built. He wore his work clothes: ample overalls, a dark shirt, steel-toed boots.

Over the course of his career, the priest had seen enough people who were hurting to know when to keep the introductions short. What will it be? he asked.

The observance of the sacraments was not what it used to be. Sunday mass and the various tests of faith had been put aside by the faithful. The rights of passage remained, as if it had been decided that life would be simplified into three distinct parts—a beginning, a middle, and an end—and that

God would handle only the beginning and the end; man would take care of the middle.

A service for my son, Marquis, a service with singing, that's what it will be, replied the Welder. No quavering. No crying. This is a man who knows exactly what death is worth, thought the priest, who got up and brought back the form.

What was the name, again?

The man looked away. The priest had to repeat himself. Marquis.

The church had set three rates, the priest explained. The Welder said that what he liked in church was the singing. He wanted singing, lots of it. The whole choir, in the nave and in the loft.

They set a date. Marquis's funeral would be held on Saturday at two o'clock in the afternoon. There would be twenty minutes of singing from the Introit to the *Libera me.*

The priest set down his pen and adopted the focused air of a confessor. The time had come to exercise his ministry, which consisted in reviving souls and presenting them to the Lord, the good and the sinful. Talk to me about Marquis, tell me what kind of Christian he was, so that I can write his eulogy.

Burnt faces lose a great deal of their natural ability to be expressive. They appear sculpted by nefarious hands. The cheeks are grafted onto the jaws. The glands atrophy so that the dry air irritates the eyes, which close in pain. The eyebrows disappear. The lips stay tightly clenched around the teeth. The words that come out of such a face are malformed and are seen as much as they are heard.

The Welder turned towards the door as if he were leaving. He stood up as if he were leaving. He nodded his head as if he were leaving. Then he sat back down, devastated.

What do you want me to say? He's dead. He could have died a lot older than he did. He could have died a lot younger, too. You don't get to decide. And if you do decide, people say you couldn't handle it. What kind of a man was he? A man like any other. A man like me. A man like you. When he was little, he raised pigeons in his grandfather's barn. He liked pigeons. Not to eat, to look at. He had up to a hundred. Later he kept bees. His grandfather showed him how to gather swarms in the trees. He was afraid to climb but he wasn't afraid of being stung. Then he sold the hives and bought rabbits. From rabbits he went to geese. He said he liked to try new things. He was good in school. When he finished high school, I wanted to teach him how to weld. But he wanted to be his own boss, not work for me. I couldn't hold that against him. He was young. He was always young. He liked women. He liked to change them often. If he had a fault, that was it: he had his fling and didn't look any further. He didn't get attached. Why? I never asked. He would show up with a new one and introduce her. Where was the last one? It was none of our business and we kept our mouths shut. He did what he wanted. The world's not like it used to be. He came home every month. He came at Christmas and on New Year's Day. He never stayed long. We would talk about what was new. We would drink a beer. He didn't talk much about himself. He would explain to his new girlfriend who was in the family and who did what. He always seemed to get along with each of them. Napierville is a small place. Once a year he would leave town. He would go to the Quebec City Carnival. He had his faults, but he also had his good qualities. He was always in a good mood. Not excited, just in a good mood. He knew how to have fun. He wasn't interested in money. Women were enough. He never told us exactly how many children he had. Never. My wife, who pays attention to the gossip, thinks there are five. I know two: one boy, one girl. He had a good friend. His name is Bob. They met at school. Bob McGreer. He's Irish. I hope he will come to the service. I know they saw each other a lot. He's an accountant in Montreal. If a guy keeps a buddy for forty years, he can't be such a bad guy— what do you think? He was lucky. A heart attack. He didn't suffer. He had a good death. He had a good life. A good life and a good death, that's enough—what do you think?

The priest watched the man get up and sit back down again. He looked more stunned than overwhelmed. He had spoken for a long time. Now the tide of words ebbed. He was suffocating.

The priest had listened, rubbing his hands and pursing his lips. What he thought, and what he preferred to keep to himself, was that the people of his parish did not know how to be sentimental. It was because of the education they had received and retained. Times had changed. They had never changed so quickly. And yet people did not seem caught off guard by modernity. They adapted very well. They worked. They built houses. They had children. They went on vacation. Then death caught up with them. Not much of a change there.

The Welder got up again, then paused with his hand on the doorknob. He would pull himself together. However devastated he might be at the loss of his second son, he had turned sixty-eight today and had raged in the void inside him long before now. He turned his ravaged face to the portraits of popes and bishops on the walls.

The priest got up. He thought he should shake his hand and he shook it.

The Welder descended the large steps of the porch. When he got to the bottom, he raised a hand to chest and staggered.

Are you alright? asked the priest.

The reply was a forced, murmured yes. In the time it took to say it, the Welder was on the ground, with his head turned to the side and his hands clutching his chest.

The priest's first thought was to go and call an ambulance.

He was just about to go when another idea crossed his mind. He felt a thrust. A real thrust, as if he had been seized from above and transported through the air. The next thing he knew was that he was on his knees beside the Welder. He made the sign of the cross over his forehead. Over his heart. Over his genitals. Over his hands and feet.

A few seconds later, the body was that of a dead man. Fate had struck a fifth time.

6

Graziella had learned that they were getting ready to build along the river to the west of Napierville. Someone with money and well-placed friends had bought a piece of land formerly reserved for agriculture and had then obtained permits from the Commission de protection du territoire agricole to build bungalows. That someone could only be Sam Samson. At Chez Gilles, they told her she could find Sam Samson at the door and window factory he had recently purchased from Yves Lazure. The factory was on the other side of the railroad tracks. She went immediately. Sam Samson wasn't there. An employee missing four fingers on one hand told her to call ahead next time instead of running all over the place. He dialed the number with what was left of his hand.

Graziella explained that she wanted to offer her services as a painter for the upcoming construction projects. She had to pay rent. She had to pay for hydro, the phone, food, clothes, school supplies, and now speech-therapy lessons for the Kid.

The conversation was short and long at the same time. Sam Samson didn't say no but he didn't say yes. He would think about it. He would see. He would call. Other than that, how was she doing?

Graziella had no trouble imagining him in front of her. He had round eyes that were close together like a racoon's, eyes that met the world without blinking and saw far, as far as the money went. She did not insist.

As soon as she left the workshop, she reproached herself for not insisting. She reproached herself for not being as sharp as Sam Samson when it came to business.

She went back through town and walked around the subdivision. She counted sixteen lots. Her accounting mind trained at the bank multiplied the number of houses by the number of rooms. It multiplied that by the number of walls and added the stairs and closets. It added up to several months of work and maybe ten thousand dollars.

Graziella needed money.

A house is more than a house—like Napierville is more than Napierville. Sam Samson built houses without ever using a hammer or circular saw or holding anything in his hand other than money to buy a contractor's licence and building permits.

He was a small man who, in the past, had worn his hair long like a hippy and worked as a professor at a *polyvalente*, a demanding job. Those who knew him at the time remembered how he was mocked openly by his students. The school was manifestly not the right place for him, and he had enough common sense to imagine a different future. Even when he had long hair, Sam Samson had been interested in activities other than pedagogy. He was arrested for trafficking illegal substances. The officer was so eager to send him to jail that he had forgotten to read him his rights, and he was pardoned. Then also he had enough common sense to imagine ending up as something other than a dealer. He cut his hair and got a job at a big store on Sainte-Catherine that isn't there anymore. He sold suits. When he became a manager, he got his first business card. Since then he was never seen without a suit and a business card. Money was his full-time job.

A house is property. People went to see Sam Samson to gain access to property. It was an important step in their lives, and no one understood better than that man how deeply seated in everyone was the desire to own a parcel of the world during their time down here. He lived in one of the most bucolic parts of Napierville, near the river. The house had been designed for a young couple that was very well off—he a tax lawyer and she an engineer—who had broken the contract and left Napierville before they'd finished building the house. As the contractor, Sam Samson had found himself with a fifteen-room palace on his hands. It offended him to live in such an extravagant house that, of course, made many people jealous, but that just about no one other than him and tax lawyers could afford. He had taken the couple to court—he was not about to let his clients think that he would not chase them to their graves if they didn't pay—but they had proven even craftier than he.

Graziella walked towards the palace, whose turrets could be seen above the trees. It was already eleven o'clock. On some days, the time was important. On that day, it was. Graziella walked fast. In front of the church, the funeral director had already placed cones to reserve all the space in front of the church for the funeral convoy.

It was an almost hot day with no wind. Fine white clouds undulated in the humid air. A jabbering host of sparrows shook the bushes. The maple trees along the Pointe des Patriotes had covered themselves in just a few days with a mountain of leaves. The dew had washed out the posters that a guy named Francis had put up. She thought about it. What to do? A few days earlier, when she had taken down one of the sheets of paper to put it in her bag, it had been out of curiosity. Now she didn't know. Or, rather, she did: the world was big and mysterious; being alone in it was not an option. A thread, a connection linked it to the people you knew and the people you didn't. This guy was someone she didn't.

She sat down on the bench where she had spent a whole summer and a whole fall sleeping and thinking. On top of the monument to Napierville's executed and exiled, a bird started singing. She recognized it: the bird without a name. She listened attentively, delighted. Then a big noisy truck came down the 219 and the bird flew off towards the pharmacy. Graziella got up and flew off, too.

In front of Côté et Paradis, the funeral home, the hearses and limousines waited in a line. Graziella imagined Marquis in the satin-lined oak box. His father had died after him. A part of Napierville gone in one fell swoop. More than the simultaneous death of the father and the son, the gossip was about the fact that Marquis's grandfather, the father of the Welder, was still alive. People wondered how he could survive such a blow at his age. In a few hours, the priest would ask God to accept his son and his grandson into the community of the dead in the sky. Lord, have mercy, is what the priest would implore. The parents, friends, and acquaintances would then accompany the bodies to the cemetery. Marquis and the Welder would have their name on the same gravestone. Two dates would tell future generations of their time in Napierville. By the standard of life expectancy in monstrously rich countries such as Canada, a relatively short time. A life cut off from the various stages of old age—old age that would at a different time have been a painful twilight but that could today seem like quasi-immortality.

Graziella crossed the bridge. The palace was directly on her right, on a slope that had had to be filled in. Whether because of a rich man's pretention or simple frugality, Sam Samson refused to take part in the competition for the nicest flower bed in Napierville. On each side of the laneway, in soil that had been brought in and barely leveled, grew couch grass, plantain grass, large bulbs of goosefoot, and ragweed.

She rang the doorbell once, and the door opened.

Yes?

Grazie could tell that the child was beginning to look like his father, and that he would look more like him as he grew older. Same eyes close together, same shifty face.

Where is your father? she asked him.

The child thought calmly for a moment. Grazie noticed that he wore a jacket and a tie like his father.

I know you, he said, you're Grazie, the crazy woman...

Grazie did not let him finish.

I know you too, she said. Where is your father?

The child thought calmly.

My father is out on business, he said.

And your mother?

This time, the child didn't stop to think.

My mother's not here either.

Then Grazie heard footsteps coming from inside the house. Maybe a younger child. Maybe a dog. Maybe a cat. She leaned in and saw an adult silhouette sneaking away. The silhouette of a racoon, she thought.

The door closed apparently all on its own. The miracle of palaces. Grazie thought: I'm not up to this. And she didn't insist.

She stopped on the bridge and leaned on the railing. The water was murky, full of silt from the dark earth. As a child, Grazie had spent a lot of time exploring both banks. The water was a companion and walking comforted her. But now she wasn't sure she was going anywhere.

She turned towards the school. The secretary recognized her and Graziella asked her to call the Kid. The secretary hesitated, wanted to get up. Grazie told her that it was important.

7

From the start of the ceremony, the Old Man saw that his whole family, down to the most distant nephews, was there. Many names escaped him, but all those people were his kin. He thought of his own death. He would have liked it to come immediately, before everyone left. If he could have said something the moment he passed to the other side, he would have said he felt worn out, that he was eager to leave his body behind. He now knew more people who were dead than living.

The funeral director brought more flowers. The men jostled and the women came forward to read each little card.

The days when the bereaved wore black from head to toe were over. The young men wore jeans and untucked shirts or t-shirts. The young women were dressed in tight pants or capris and coloured jerseys that hugged their pretty breasts.

Someone took the Old Man's arm to sit him down on one of the strawberry-coloured couches. He wanted to say that he needed a coffin, not a couch.

A joke. But this was not the time for jokes. He said that he wanted to stay standing like everyone else.

A man with a beard approached to offer his condolences. Together they looked at the deceased in their coffins. The bearded man moved his lips. He was looking for something to say. He was relieved when he found it, and repeated a few times that the embalmer did a great job. The Old Man felt himself grow a few centuries older.

Then it was the turn of a young woman with a child. He recognized her without being sure exactly what place she occupied in the family. She didn't seem to know either. She shook the Old Man's hand. Then, thinking better of it, she kissed his cheek. She had warm lips, warm breath. With one hand on the Old Man's shoulder, she started speaking quickly in a soft voice. Usually the Old Man would shake his head and point to his hearing aids to indicate that he was deaf as a post. This time he let the warm lips and the warm breath be. He had been deaf for long enough to have lost faith in language, but besides his hearing loss and his sometimes unwitting, sometimes deliberate muteness, he suffered from none of the infirmities that affected very old men, and he looked with rapture on her warm red lips as the words poured out of them.

Death came and went, and he remained. He was one hundred and two years and seven months old. The fact that he was one hundred and two years and seven months old was all you needed to know about who he was and what he expected from the future. In half a year he would be one hundred and three. Which would be of no importance. At one hundred, a man had usually found his place in the shadows. But not him. He speculated. When? When was the last step? The last rainbow? The last handshake? Tomorrow? The next day? He had to be next in line for the cemetery. His vigour had turned against him. His hands were covered in liver spots. He stood with his back bent like all old men who had worked hard. Under his wild eyebrows, his prune-coloured eyes seemed to be on the lookout for the fighting force of life. It was there. It was there. It was still there. But he wasn't up to it anymore. Eventually life would land a great blow, and the world he had built would topple.

The next woman who approached him and kissed his cheek was a mere sixty-something. She wrinkled her forehead and smiled. She was the sister of his daughter-in-law, the wife of the Welder. Two pretty women. She reminded him so much of their mother, another pretty woman.

A little later, a group of children invaded the room. They were the ones his grandson Marquis drove to school in the morning and home in the evening. Someone must have whispered to them that the old, hobbled man was one hundred and two years old and that today he was burying his son and his grandson. They whispered amongst themselves, and turned around to look curiously at the old man as they filed two-by-two past the man they had only ever known behind the steering wheel of the school bus.

Another woman came to kiss his cheek. She presented a great grandson to him. He recognized her. She had gotten a bit bigger, but her skin was just as lovely. To her child she explained that the old man was the last father he had left. A father far away in time, tired, bent, deaf, but a father he could count on. His mother took off his cap and told him to shake his great grandfather's hand. He did.

Later, the priest arrived with his stole around his neck and a little black book in his hand. Raising his arms, he turned around a few times to obtain silence. All the mouths stopped moving, and he read from the little book. Lord, have mercy. Lord, have mercy. Lord, have mercy. Joining his hands, he continued with the traditional prayers known only to those over the age of fifty. A murmur rose from the congregation. The Old Man recognized the chorus of responses mumbled behind rosary beads. He offered up his own. He kissed the cross. He looked at the shiny black beads that had faded overtime. His rosary was one of the few things in his possession that was as old as he was. He had received it at the age of six for his first communion. He had kept it under his pillow nearly ever since. When he couldn't sleep, he would take it out and recite his prayers in the dark without really praying. When he put on his coat, he took the beads from out of his pillow and put it in his chest pocket with his handkerchief. A good luck charm and spokesperson.

Then the congregation left. The final minutes were reserved for close family. The Old Man was surrounded by his six daughters. One took him by the arm and together they approached the prie-dieu.

Again he got the feeling that his reign was coming to an end. He was a survivor. Survivors are the dead that are still standing, he thought.

Tenderly he put his hand on the forehead of his son, the Welder. He did the same for his grandson, Marquis. His thoughts were simple. A man does what a man does. A woman does what a woman does. The result, if there is one, is called a newborn. That newborn is given a name—just one for its entire life, along with one or two nicknames, occasionally. When it becomes an adult, this newborn in turn does what a man does, or what a woman does. They call it a love story, and regardless of how much love or story is involved, it ensures that human life continues a little while longer. It had been this way since Adam and Eve. Nothing complicated. Him. Her. A unique combination, to which was now added the evolution of species and the survival of the fittest. Then one day every man, woman, and ancestor in the long line of reproducers disappeared and ended up six feet underground.

The funeral director closed the coffins. The porters came forward. They first took out flowers to attach to the limousine.

The funeral procession came around the Pointe des Patriotes to stop in front of the church. The priest waited on the steps with his four altar boys.

Napierville had been a wealthy parish that had done well by its successive vicars. Its church was large and could hold around a thousand believers. At the top of the wood columns painted to look like marble were shining gilded acanthus leaves.

Once the coffins were placed on biers and brought to the transept, the porters returned to the porch, beyond the fonts.

Graziella and the Kid entered the large room during the reading of the epistle. Saint Paul was addressing the

Thessalonians. He was telling them that on the day God came down to earth, the dead would be resurrected to eternal life, and the living would join them in the sky. The deacon was supporting herself with both hands on the lectern. When she had trouble with certain words longer than two syllables, she stopped and furrowed her brow. When she had regained her breath, her voice thundered in the loudspeakers. God was God. Sinners were sinners. The dead were the dead. Eternal life was eternal life.

After the reading of the epistle, the church fell silent. Swaying on her large legs, the woman walked from the lectern to her seat in the choir. The priest rose. He looked perplexed, and he paused for a long moment before beginning the alleluia.

The Kid had never set foot in a church. All he knew about the religion of his ancestors was what he had been taught at school. What he remembered mostly was the story of Adam and Eve in paradise and how they had been tricked by the serpent with the apple. For this insignificant gluttony, God chewed them out and banished them from the garden forever. Either Genesis was the story of people's fears without commentary, or the Almighty did exist and He did not have a sense of humour. The Kid had talked about it with his mother. She was not a great fan of stories of fear, but she acknowledged that the story was, at least, simple. Any more simple and it wouldn't be a story. A couple, an enchanted garden, a devil, an apple… eat it or don't. She also acknowledged its staying power. It had traversed continents and generations and become a part of history. Once you learned its conclusion, you didn't forget it. God had reserved the right to decide and He had decided. One judgement for all. From the beginning of time until the end of time. Now all that was left was for each person to earn, in their short life, their own safe passage to the palace in the sky of an easily offended God. And this safe passage was guaranteed to no one.

But in hindsight, it was easy to spot the holes in the story. What about luck? What about evolution? What about geological forces at work well before Adam and Eve were ever around? What about the dinosaurs? And eighty million galaxies? And past civilizations? And competing religions?

The priest sang with his arms in the air. The faithful answered. The Kid was fascinated. He wanted to get closer to what was happening up at the front. The promise of the resurrection of the dead and the ascension into the sky had made a great impression on him. He asked his mother if he could go up. Grazie indicated that he could go up as far as he liked. Obviously her mind was on something other than the ceremony, and the Kid went all the way to the transept, the waiting room of paradise.

For years Graziella had repressed what had happened between her and Marquis. The momentum had faded for both of them. Today her past was rushing in at her and her head was pounding. She was falling to pieces. Her heart was beating erratically. Grazie felt an urgent need to impose some order on this restlessness.

Of all the people she had met in her life, Marquis was the one she had understood best. You want me, I want you. Communion wasn't the right word. She remembered afternoons spent in a hotel room on the highway. They didn't talk much. She was attracted. He was attracted. Where did this attraction come from? she had once asked. Marquis didn't ask himself those questions. He didn't answer them, either. He used a few ready-made sentences, which he adapted to the circumstances. Even more often he used monosyllables. A narrow path of monosyllables. Graziella had gone to look in her own mind. The two of them had been as close as you could be. Being so close had changed her on the inside. Not him.

When he left for other affairs, he had said what all men say when they get the urge to leave: don't wait for me.

She had done what many women do when they feel so close to a man: she had waited. One month. Two months. Six months. She was pregnant.

One day when she was begging as usual outside the grocery store, a woman with a briefcase had approached her, saying in all seriousness that she was paid to approach her because she was begging, because she was pregnant, because she and the baby needed help and society helped the people who needed it.

They went together to the new CLSC in the expanded pharmacy building.

A doctor examined her.

She had to answer questions about her past, her present, her future. Was she sick? Depressed? Suicidal? What was in her head? What was she thinking about? A box for each part of her being.

These people were serious. Grazie wanted this child. They would not leave her alone. Behind the closed doors, she got scared.

She had thought about disappearing. Not like Marquis, who had never really disappeared, but like those tireless people who, instead of staying in one place, simply hit the road as if they were the road. Today she would have told the doctor and the social worker sitting behind their desks that the priest, in his big gilded church beside his ten-room rectory, he knew how to beg.

In the end she had accepted society's help. With her social-assistance money she had rented a small house that no one wanted. The child was born. She had looked for a job that would let her be with him all the time. Sometimes she passed the ghost of Marquis, and he gave her a few dollars.

The service was ending. Graziella wondered whether she would follow the funeral procession all the way to the cemetery.

The Kid was meandering from pew to pew in the large aisle. When he turned around and looked at her, she gestured that he should come back, but he shook his head no. She thought that someday soon he would only do what he wanted. She would no longer be a mother. He would no longer be a child.

People went up to receive communion. Solemn singing filled the church.

Graziella saw the Kid touch the two coffins as he walked by. He moved well. He seemed comfortable, even when he was out of place, like at that moment. It was speaking that gave him trouble. The words didn't come out. Several times the school principal had mentioned speech therapy, exercises. She had given her a name and a phone number. The school did what it could, but it wasn't enough. Grazie imagined a problem in his throat, a dented wheel that a well-paid speech therapist could repair. She had called and said that she had no money. The speech therapist had been accommodating. The sessions had begun. She was waiting to see the results.

The people in line for communion looked away. Graziella gestured to the Kid, but he didn't see her. He was looking at the Old Man in the front row. Tense, bloodless. Wrinkles, eyes, a nose, a mouth, but no more vitality.

After the rituals with the incense and the sprinkling of water on the dead in their coffins, the porters came up the aisle. The procession formed behind them.

The Kid appeared suddenly between the pews. W-w-wher-re a-are they t-taking them? he wanted to know. To the cemetery. Do you want to go?

They went. On the way, Graziella explained what she knew about cemeteries, the land that the society of the living consigned to the society of the dead, a meeting place, a place of peace, or rest and eternity, with no distinction between good and bad, where each gravestone bore a name, date of birth, and date of death, and sometimes an epitaph, just a few words, no more, like when you take a holiday, because life was complicated enough, with its tears and lamentations, without adding the problems of the dead.

The limousines turned to the right and stopped in front of the giant cross. The porters got out and took out the coffins to lay them on the straps. The priest said a prayer while liberally sprinkling water from his aspergillum into the large hole in the ground bordered by synthetic grass. Lord, have mercy! Lord, have mercy! Lord, have mercy!

The Old Man had gotten even older. His deep wrinkles were now like a mask over his face. His field of vision was shrinking. But he could still see that, beyond the cemetery, the fields were full of corn. Fine humid-green shoots in straight parallel lines stretching towards infinity. It was simple and beautiful, like a drawing. Human beings were good with lines, drawings, and volumes. It was no surprise that they planted their dead in rows like onions underneath stone guardians.

The Old Man bent over. With great difficulty he took a handful of dirt and let it fall to the bottom of the hole. The coffins sounded hollow, as if their occupants had disappeared. If agony made a sound, that was it: a low vibration that sliced through the silence he had been living in for years.

The Old Man stood up, his mouth blocked up by the pain. He came from another time, a rudimentary time, discontinuous, a memory for every event. But it was not yet a tomb. He sensed something, something only foreseen by those who, like him, had cheated death: that life, not death, is the real surprise.

A hand touched him. A hand that, because of the frivolous way it touched him, could only be that of a child. The Old Man looked for the hand. It was the Kid's. He took it and pressed it warmly between his. As far back as his memories stretched, there had always been hands in his hands, just as there had always been fantastic creatures in his dreams.

His mother's hands. The hands of his older brothers and older sisters. The hands of wives. The hands of children. Of grandchildren. Of great grandchildren. Warm links in a chain.

The Kid withdrew his hand. He bent over the grass carpet and took a good handful of earth. Standing at the edge of the hole, he lifted it over his head and threw it down as hard as he could.

8

During the summer Francis rarely went into town. He got up at dawn, fed the cows, milked them, checked to see that they were in good health, and fed the calves. After lunch, he got down to the drudgery of dealing with the manure and then, if the weather was good, he went out to the fields. There was always something to do in the fields. Anyone even slightly inclined towards perfectionism could spend days out there. You had to know how to stop. At five o'clock, he went back to the barn. Fed the cows again, milked them again. Examined them again, too. A farmer in his barn was like a caregiver in a hospital: he looked, he felt, he interpreted. Francis was still thinking about what had happened to Bonté III, what had happened to so many others before her. A cow's life was full of challenges. At eight o'clock, sometimes at nine o'clock if he was running late, he could smoke a cigarette and say to himself: another day's work done. Often he would take off his boots and sleep right there in the loft. His father, in his day, had done the same, as had no doubt his whole line of ancestors who had bent over backwards to carve out a corner of the land. One thing was clear: those who left the cows and the fields in search of a less demanding life never came back. And another thing: after a day's work, there was still the night.

On the answering machine, the first message said: Hello... I saw your ad... We could meet tomorrow... five o'clock... at the playground in town. Then a phone number. Great, he thought: great: the clear, affirmative voice of someone who says when and where. Good!

He called and left his own message: Hello... five o'clock is too early... I have to take care of my cows... let's say nine o'clock... what's your name? Call me back.

In the next message, the voice sounded more relaxed. Tomorrow had become Saturday at nine, and the village playground had become the Pointe de Patriotes.

That's a funny place to fall in love. There's never anyone there. I won't have to worry about picking the wrong woman, thought Francis. He was intrigued. He called back: Ok, Saturday at nine sounds good. What's your name?

He waited for a reply that never came.

To help him prepare for the harvest, Francis had hired a young neighbour. He was big, tall, strong as a horse, and well meaning, but he was all thumbs and had a strange attitude towards the cows. There was no way to convince him that a cow was hospitality incarnate, that for a cow, the most important being on the planet was not another cow, but the person taking care of her. It wasn't that the boy was afraid, but he stayed as far away from the cows as possible, and when he did approach them, it was with his arms in front of him, ready to move away at the slightest suspicious movement.

The cows sensed this circumspection. They would stop chewing and look up, observing him with their big eyes. This made him even more hesitant. An untimely vicious circle. Francis told him that he would get used to them, and the cows to him, but deep down he didn't really believe it.

Two of the animals were lame. They stayed on the ground and ate less than the others, which affected their production. The veterinarian had examined them. One had an ulcer on its sole. The vet had trimmed the hoof and soaked it in a medicated solution. The other, Bonté III's sister, had a problem in her front right knee. She needed space and a chance to walk.

Saturday, before his date at the Pointe des Patriotes in town, Francis himself bathed the hoof of the cow with the ulcer. He left his employee to take the other one for a walk at the end of a rope, and hurried inside. He showered. He shaved. The drain in the sink seemed partially clogged. Francis cleaned the trap, filled the bowl, and watched it empty more slowly than it should have. His mother hadn't said anything. She was usually quick to pester him about these minor domestic details.

She had figured it out from the signs, even before the voicemails. One of her sisters, who lived in front of the mill, had called her. They had chatted: the cows, the fields, the tractor maintenance, the equipment, the buildings, the house—did a man in his situation have time for a woman? One day, when Francis was getting ready to milk the cows, the door had swung open. What was he thinking? she had snapped. He had listened to her be right. Nothing he didn't already know. He said nothing. Then he turned on the compressor, and when the noise from the machine filled the room, his poor mother was forced to shut up.

He put on a shirt, a pair of pants, and fancy shoes that hurt his feet. He didn't have any others. It had been a long day. His young assistant had misjudged his swing and hit a tree with the hay rake. An hour and a half running back and forth unscrewing bolts, welding broken parts, and making up for the lost time.

His mother was waiting for him downstairs in the living room. He saw her disapproving face turn towards the television, her finger turn up the volume on the remote. She said nothing. He said nothing. Outside, in the evening, a part of the past was waiting for him. It stung. Smells, hair, body parts. He had met Huguette when he was sixteen, just before his father died. It had lasted a few years and went nowhere. He was still hurt.

He got into the pickup, backed up, and set straight out towards town. He saw his employee walking the cow at the end of a rope in front of the barn. He waved.

In his headlights, he saw a green truck loaded with bales of hay. It was Clémont. Clémont had gotten lucky the first time. Now there were two of them, he and his wife, to work sixteen hours a day on the farm.

His beautiful Huguette, on the other hand, managed a boss's schedule and answered the phone somewhere in Alberta, while the man she had chosen for a husband operated a giant hydraulic shovel, mixing the northern oil sands to extract Canadian oil. What she had told Francis ten years earlier, when he had proposed that they be a couple and work together, was no, you will not have me, I'll never lock myself in Napierville with the cows. He had seen a woman's realism, an aspiration for a better life, which excluded a good part of Napierville: the cows, the fields, the dirt, the sweat, the isolation.

Out of habit, he took the Daunais-Decoigne bridge. His paternal grandmother used to live out that way, in the white house with a veranda under the gable. How is it that you know someone? She had died when Francis was nine years old, but he cherished her still. Something about her. A way of living. He remembered her hair, the shape of her glasses, the scar on her lower lip from a canker the doctors had cut out, the long white aprons, the white shoes, them too, the ones she often asked him to undo and tie up again so they would not be so tight. There was a picture of her as a young woman on the wall in the family room, standing in a flower-print dress with a bouquet of flowers under her neck. He had not known that woman; why did he feel like he knew her better than he knew many members of his own family? She existed. She would always exist.

Francis parked his pickup in front of the building on Rue Saint-Jacques where the notary, the dentist, and the accountant had their offices. He looked at his watch. There was no hurry. He had ten minutes to think, to buy a pack of cigarettes and put it in his pocket without opening it. The Pointe des Patriotes was just two minutes away, past the post office.

Three large tractor-trailers were crossing the Grégoire bridge. The light turned red and they stopped. Francis recognized the smell. He even heard the squeals: hee! hee! heeee! Many dairy farmers like him had sold their herds to raise pigs for the reason, good or bad, that pigs fattened up and made it to the abattoir quickly and almost on their own; no need to get close to them or touch them twice a day, talk to them, worry about how they were doing. You had free time. Dairy farmers, on the other hand, had only a few short minutes to think about what it would be like to have free time, to dream, to let their minds wander. What did he want? A cigarette, first of all. He felt the pack in his pocket and took a deep breath. The idea that cigarettes were poisonous had finally entered his head. He had stopped. Now he sucked on lozenges or chewed on his cheek when he didn't have any. Seriously, what did he want? To be sixteen again would be wonderful. He was thirty-two, twice sixteen. A life in two parts, dangling over the middle. What did he want? The free time of a pork farmer, or a way, if one existed, to tie all the parts of his life into a unified whole.

The construction holidays had come. Two weeks without pay. In the morning, the Kid went across the road to play in the school yard. He had made a friend, and that friend brought a skipping rope, an old scooter, lollipops, and cans of orangeade.

Being outside gave him some colour. His arms and his legs were tanned. The pool was a little farther, past the school. Graziella took him there in the afternoon. His friend's name was Juanita. Over dinner it was n-nni-ita this, n-nni-ita that.

Grazie had asked what Juanita's father's name was, what her mother's name was, where they came from, what they did. The Kid didn't know anything. He was only interested in p-pla-aying. Grazie told herself that he had a right to the better parts of life.

After the two weeks of the construction holidays, Sam Samson, the contractor, was nowhere to be found, and Phil Fournier, the person she had been working for since the spring, wasn't calling anymore. On the corkboard at the grocery store, Grazie posted a flyer where she had written, at the top of the page, Small Painting Jobs, in the middle, her name, and at the bottom, her phone number, on snipped ends you could tear off. Every day she went by to see if the ad was still there, between the cars to be sold and the puppies to be adopted. It was still there, but it was evidently not big enough. She would have needed an immense panel to draw the attention of Napierville to a painter who was just trying to feed herself and her child.

She wasn't out of money yet, but she was in trouble. Something wasn't working. She had no reason to feel scared, just a sense, an intuition, that knowing how and being willing to work was not enough. She went on long walks. She walked past worksites that had reopened after the holidays and where the work was now almost done, past others where work had just started. A stranger had taken her place in Napierville. Someone who no doubt painted faster for less money. She was happier not knowing who.

She walked by the bank, a branch of the one she had worked for in Montreal.

When she returned, her throat dry, from her walks, she went straight for her telephone and her precious answering machine. Then she drank a large glass of water. She started thinking about her past, her father, her mother, her two sisters, the happy household she'd had as a child. Grazie had been eight years old, her sisters twelve, when their father had lost his job in Saint-Jean. The factory was closing. The girls never knew what he did. He just said "job." He said "grinder," "switch," and "wrench." "Floats" for trucks came out of the "shop." He never did find another real job. He was a peddler. He delivered groceries. Every fall he packaged vegetables in a warehouse. In the winter he shoveled snow. Grazie remembered a father who was always in a good mood, who was convinced that the brutality of the world ended at the front door, who played cards with his friends, teased his girls telling them nonsensical stories about a poor, wandering king who ate turnips, a goat that climbed trees, and fence posts and stones that told the king and the goat where to go. Grazie was fifteen when he lost his footing on a stepladder and shattered his skull on the cement paving stone. Just bad luck, he would have said, had he still been able to open his mouth and tell his absurd stories. Grazie's sisters had gone off to work. Their mother had moved in with another man. Grazie had started to dream of a life just for herself, just like, as a child, she had dreamed of things just for herself—a toy, a stuffed animal, a hat. How could she not be nostalgic? She had, alternately and beyond measure, begun to hate each member of her family. Then she moved away from them and into a world where loving and hating were complex and exhausting.

Who was she? Did she still dream? She asked herself these questions as she prepared the Kid's favourite meal: buttered macaroni, cheese, tomato sauce. She heard laughter and turned around. It was Juanita and the Kid. They were hungry. Grazie kept a small portion for herself.

The next day, the Kid asked if he could eat at Juanita's house. He returned at dusk. She asked him what he ate. He didn't know. Was it good? He answered with a nod and a smile.

She went to bed, even though she didn't feel like sleeping. Finally, she fell asleep. She woke hours later to screams and gunshots from the television in the kitchen. She had trouble breathing, had trouble moving her feet. This had happened to her before, as a child, and then later, when she worked for the bank. She felt like she was unravelling. She yelled to the kitchen. The Kid lowered the volume on the television. She got up. She slapped her cheeks in the mirror a couple of times.

It was very hot. During the day she had brought the Kid and Juanita to have a picnic under the trees in the school-yard, then to the pool.

The next day was Friday. The heat wave in Napierville continued. Even though it was early, she went back to see Sam Samson. She talked to Phil Fournier. They both told her that it wasn't a good time. Maybe later, in the fall.

On her way back, she stopped at the bank. There, too, a contractor had installed a fence, a sign, and machines for digging and lifting. There were piles of dirt, beams, yellow insulation, stone blocks, and bricks on skids, workers wearing hardhats and t-shirts wet from sweat. She asked a bricklayer where the foreman was. With his trowel, he pointed to a paunchy man, busy behind the door of this truck on the phone.

She waited in the sun in front of the truck. When he finally covered his phone with his hand and half closed his eye as if to say what do you want, hun, make it quick, she approached and said what she had to say.

Hello. I'm looking for work. I'm a painter.

The man's face stayed as it was, half way between vexed and disinterested.

I have all the employees I need here.

But I need work. I have to pay rent. I have a kid to feed.

He let out a long sigh and chased Grazie from his mind.

Sorry.

Grazie suddenly felt very hot, feverish. She went home, breathing laboriously, sweat running down her face. Something wasn't working. There was no more Napierville, no more country, no more humanity at all, just a high wall: banks and contractors on one side, on the other, the multitude of workers like her, with their meager tools for survival: work permits, trowels, hammers, paintbrushes. She saw the moment approach when she would no longer know what to do or where to go, when she would raise her head and look to the right, to the left, then start again, to the right, to the left, until she succumbed to exhaustion, like an inch worm.

9

Are you…?
Yes.

Francis.

Graziella.

When she saw someone approaching quickly from the
other side of the memorial, slightly hunched, arms swing-
ing, shirtsleeves rolled up to his elbows, she thought: man
seeks woman. Then she had turned it around in her mind:
woman seeks man. Dreams colliding. They were on equal
footing.

We could shake hands…

If you like.

He was as he'd described himself on the poster: average
height, thin but sturdy, blond hair, stooped neck, rings under
his eyes.

We could go somewhere…

No, I like it here.

Alright, but if you change your mind…

He leaned against the monument.

Are you sure? We could go to the bar; there's a patio at
the back.

Another time.

He looked at her and, for the first time, instead of speaking, he smiled.

Grazie had to admit that she did not feel great about the situation. She wanted to get out of there. She felt uncomfortable in a way that she could not stand for long. Better tell him right away that there was a child in the picture.

A boy? a girl?

A boy. He will be ten soon.

Great!

Grazie waited. No further reply came.

What do you mean?

Great. That's what I said.

Grazie agreed: great. But that didn't mean it was simple.

It's not easy, she said.

I should have brought forms, you know, like the ones matchmaking companies use. We could have filled them out and compared our answers. What you like… What you don't… What I like… What I don't… Favourite colour. Liberal or PQ?

Except it's much too dark to fill out forms…

They felt better, better enough to stand there and look at each other without feeling like they were observing each other through binoculars like exotic birds.

She had asked around. At the restaurant, Gilles had told her that there was no better cattle farmer in Napierville. At the hardware store, where she got her paint, tape, rollers, and paintbrushes, Georges had agreed wholeheartedly: no one in Napierville raises better Holsteins. At the library, where she brought the Kid and his friend Juanita, Gisele's face had lit up: of course I know him, he's my cousin! He raises the best Holsteins…

If he was the best at anything, he wasn't talking about it. Grazie thought she understood: outside of a barn or a farming competition, a man who raised cows had no interest in bragging. Other farmers, townspeople, even her father, who

rarely had a bad word to say about anyone, said they were
idiots.

Don't just stand there, sit down.

He looked in the air. He shuffled, which made the shadows around him move like ripples in water. In the end he
stayed standing, his arms at his side like two handles on a
vase, his thumbs hooked into his pockets. He looked like a
guy who was not annoyed.

I hear you raise cattle.

That's right, yes.

How many do you have?

It depends on the year: thirty-some, never more than
forty.

Is that a lot? Or not many?

It depends.

On what?

On how you take care of them.

Do you like it?

It depends.

She was impressed, but also very confused: here was
someone who lived with cows, who fed them, took care of
them, milked them and sold their milk, took care of their
calves. A kind of shepherd.

Question by question, Francis shook himself awake and
walked around the monument, then went to sit by Graziella.

I wonder if it was hard on them.

Who are you talking about?

He gestured to the monument.

The ones they deported to Australia: four months in a
sailboat. Can you imagine?

He shook his head and pursed his lips, imagining the
long voyage, the forced labour, returning to your family after
five years.

She had told him about the Kid. Now did she have to tell him that there was a time when she had spent her nights and much of her days here, at this miniature historical site, with no company but the names of the two men hanged at the Pied-du-Courant prison in Montreal and the dozen deported to Australia, a time when, like the people of Napierville whose houses, barns, and harvests had been burnt, she used to ask herself: what country am I living in? What happened? I see nothing, I feel nothing, I understand nothing, and I don't want to know anything. I'm struggling. Is this madness? Short madness, like exile, or long madness, like death? I would pay dearly for the night to be over.

So tell me, Francis, why the poster? Why not an ad in the *Journal de Montréal*? Or online? I feel like all of Napierville is watching us.

Let them watch!

Other than me, who called?

No one else.

No one?

No.

In that case…

You're right, we're stuck together. Great, eh!

He laughed heartily and stood up.

Come on, he said.

Grazie understood that he was not going to give up. It would work or it wouldn't. Dance clubs, bars, movie theatres, plays, restaurants, everything that had been invented to standardize encounters between men and women, orient what passed for conversation, and bring two strangers close enough to make them presentable to each other, he wanted that for them. In Napierville, other than the restaurant Chez Gilles, there was only the bar, so they went there.

Grazie watched Francis. He held the glass in one hand and the bottle in the other, taking short sips from both containers. Grazie had seen drunks at work. He wasn't one of them.

This was the second time they had met at the bar. Grazie imagined dozens of others, same place, same time. The bar, which had been there for ages, seemed to be the best Napierville had to offer to people with no communication skills, possibly because of its name: Le Voyageur, a Bill-101 translation of The Traveller's.

From the raised patio they watched heat lightning dance across the horizon.

We should do something, you and me.

We are doing something.

When you say it like that...

Francis drank a mouthful of beer, looked around, sniffed the air.

Phew!

He was bothered by the smell from the factory, which stagnated over the town on windless nights. He shook his head. Do something to take his mind off it, thought Grazie.

Do you think a storm is coming?

I hope not.

While he explained at length why a storm is never good for the field—too much water at once, too much wind— Grazie saw a short fat man get up from the table where he was sitting alone and totter towards them.

Francis was just getting to the merits of furrows, ditches, and underground drainage, when the short fat man, tears in his eyes, gave him something like a friendly punch on the shoulder. Then he laughed, a drunken laugh.

Look who it is: Mystique, in the flesh! exclaimed Francis.

Moving slowly and looking lost, the man named Mystique moved towards a chair.

He had reached that state of drunkenness where space shrinks and bodies, tables, and chairs blur together in a thick fog.

Is he often like this?

Francis looked at his watch.

At this time of day, yes.

What's his problem?

Low morale—depression, as they say. It's in his family: his mother, his grandmother, his aunts and uncles, his cousins. Come on, let's bring him home.

Grazie remembered being disappointed, but not like this. Francis led inside from the patio then through the stools and tables. There was no one there except customers for whom beer and a girl dancing under an orange light went hand in hand.

My name's not Mystique, said Mystique, stopping at the bottom of the stairs.

You can't even remember your real name, said Francis.

My name's not Mystique.

A thin smile made his badly shaven face almost handsome. Forehead smooth, mouth half open, he was happy and sad, sad and happy: someone was talking to him, someone was listening to him. Francis opened the door of his truck.

Get in, he said.

I want a beer.

Get in.

Francis waited. There was no need to guide him. He did what he was told, at least when there was someone to tell him what to do. He managed to get over the step and sit down.

I want a beer.

Tomorrow, tomorrow…

Suddenly, hot rain started to fall. First a few drops, then a torrent.

Heh, heh, heh…

Mystique's eyes closed and he fell asleep like a sack between the two of them. Francis slowly crossed the bridge and continued on.

This isn't the first time someone's taken him home, explained Francis.

Why is he called Mystique?

Francis shrugged. He didn't know the answer. Probably a childhood joke that Mystique had never been able to shake off.

They crossed the train tracks. A large truck was in front of them with all the lights on around its trailer. It sucked up the rain and flung it off behind in whirlwinds. Soon it turned off to the left. Francis accelerated, but he quickly had to slow down because of how much the tires were slipping on the wet ground.

What were you saying? asked Grazie.

Me? Nothing.

Don't dodge the question. You were saying that you and I should do something.

Oh yeah, you're right, I did say that. We could start by waking up Mystique, we're almost there.

Do you mean leave him on the side of the road?

No, no, he lives here.

He turned left and honked the horn.

You're here, Mystique; party's over.

Francis shoved him. He grimaced: either he was having a nightmare, or the mix of alcohol and the medication he had taken were twisting his stomach.

Come on, said Grazie, quietly, come on.

He opened and closed his hands a few times, stretching out his fingers and thumbs.

Francis and Grazie were holding him up when someone came out of the house. In the blur of the headlights and the rain, the resemblance between brother and sister was striking. Same round head, same sad smile. Except that the sister was sober, solid enough for both of them. She took Grazie's place. Francis stayed to help him up the stairs. When he got back in the truck, he was soaked to the skin.

Great, he said, great, and started to undress.

Grazie said that she preferred a bed to a sticky car seat. Francis went back to town and turned left. It was still raining torrentially, and the noise took the place of the conversation. In front of the house, they took in the deluge for a moment. Then they hurried inside.

In the kitchen, an old woman watched them go by, glancing occasionally into the corner with the giant television. The woman said nothing. Francis said nothing.

Now the bed was empty. Grazie went to the window and opened the blinds. It was not yet morning, more the orange-mauve colour of dawn. The rain had stopped. When? The babble of the starlings and the sparrows came in through the open window. As did an odour, more sour than floral, not really unpleasant. Earth, water, plants, manure. She inhaled it several times with shallow breaths.

Where was Francis at this hour? Had he only slept for five minutes? She remembered the two of them lying there.

Do you want pillows? You may as well be comfortable.
Yes.
The two of them lying there during the night.
Grazie opened a closet, took out a pair of jeans that were much too big for her and darned at the knees, a long shirt, and boots without laces.

Great! Give me your hand.
When she had dressed and put on the boots, she went downstairs. By the kitchen sink, the woman, no doubt his mother, turned to look at her. Grazie waited for a question, a hello, any sign, but nothing came. The kitchen opened onto a mud room. She closed the door softly.

What is it?
My hand.
And that?
…
And that?

No need to be an anatomy specialist. Grazie opened her legs. Face-to-face.

Outside, the pickup was parked in front of the shed. She found her clothes, his too, in two piles on either side of the steering wheel.

Softly, softly…

Grazie didn't feel so young anymore. Nothing sudden. Calm for her alone.

She was surprised by the smell of the barn. She pushed the air out of her lungs. She kept herself from inhaling for a long time, until she felt dizzy.

The cows were tied up in two long rows facing white-washed walls. Their one activity seemed to be putting their mouths into the brown-green vegetable mixture and swallowing. Grazie got the feeling she wasn't interrupting. A cat jumped towards her from a below a window. It sat down, stared at her, then dashed off between the cows' legs.

The Kid had slept at his aunt's house. Grazie had half lied to him, telling him that she wasn't there because she couldn't avoid it. How many times would she lie to him in the future?

She continued on, looking at each animal. Gueules plates, as they were sometimes called. Each one had an identifying tag around its neck. How many were there? He had said between thirty and forty. There seemed to be a hundred, all standing, wide awake, eyes alert.

Grazie was examining the way their tails twitched when she finally saw Francis. He attached the milking machine in his hand to a bar above his head, disappeared between two cows, and then came out from behind the other side of the trough. He was in a hurry.

About another two hours, he said, kissing her on the mouth.

He went back between two cows, took the milking machine, hunched down, and attached the cups of the machine.

She understood that milking involved running from one animal to the next, crouching down, grabbing the udder, washing the teat, attaching the machine, standing up, running again, crouching again, detaching the machine from the first cow, getting up, crouching down, working like a madman. You needed a good back, a good eye, and fast hands.

When the milking compressor shut off, Grazie was waiting outside. It was mid-morning. Francis joined Grazie under the tree. They talked about cows. They couldn't learn anything, they couldn't teach you anything, but they gave you milk and manure, and they were good company.

On the road, several cars slowed as they passed by. Grazie said that she felt like all of Napierville knew and was watching.

Great! said Francis.

Literary Translation

The *Literary Translation* series publishes English or French translations of contemporary or classic works in various literary genres, chosen for their unique qualities from the Canadian and international literary corpus.

Series editors:

Marc Charron and Luise von Flotow

Recent titles:

Laurence, Margaret. *De l'autre côté du Jourdain*. Trans. Caroline Lavoie. 2015.

Myre, Suzanne. *Death Sentences*. Trans. Cassidy Hildebrand. 2014.

Shields, Carol. *Le Carnaval du quotidien*. Trans. Élise Fournier Lévêque. 2014.

Molina Lora, Luis, and Julio Torres-Recinos, eds. *Cloudburst: An Anthology of Hispanic Canadian Short Stories*. Trans. dir. Hugh Hazelton. 2013.

Saidullah, Ahmad. *Le Bonheur et autres troubles*. Trans. Annick Geoffroy-Skuce, Marc Charron, and Caroline Lavoie. 2013.

Tawada, Yoko. *Portrait of a Tongue: An Experimental Translation*. Trans. Chantal Wright. 2013.

Wolf, Christa. *They Divided the Sky: A Novel*. Trans. Luise Von Flotow. 2013.

Glennon, Paul. *Le Dodécaèdre ou Douze cadres à géometrie variable*. Trans. dir. Marc Charron and Julie Stéphanie Normandin. 2010.

www.press.uottawa.ca

Printed in November 2015
at Imprimerie Gauvin,
Gatineau (Québec), Canada.